Back to Thule

VALERIO GARGIULO

ISBN 978-9935-24-582-3

DEDICATION

This book is dedicated to the memory of Father
Gioacchino Santoro (1911-2007).

CONTENTS

Acknowledgments   i

1   Between Three Eras   1

2   Premonitions, Dreams and Ghosts   18

3   Everything Flows   38

4   *Pavor Nocturnus*   56

5   The World Up And Down   77

6   The Pact   92

7   Interconnected Worlds   110

8   Séance   123

9   The Other Dimension   133

10   Every Phantom, A Destiny   146

ACKNOWLEDGEMENTS

This book was made possible by the many people who inspired and supported me in numerous ways. I am grateful for the support and guidance provided by my daughter Aurora, my parents Ciro and Elvira, my girlfriend Anna, my aunt Adele and my brothers Cristiano and Paolo. I want to thank also Brunella Voto, Roberto Cuorvo, IÐA Zimsen, Dario Farruggia, Cristina Presti, Vitale Fusco, Marco Perrotta, Silja Pálmarsdóttir, Gianluca Noci Candelas, Joseph Lovecchio, Giuseppe Filodoro and Pippo Messina for their feedback and contributions.

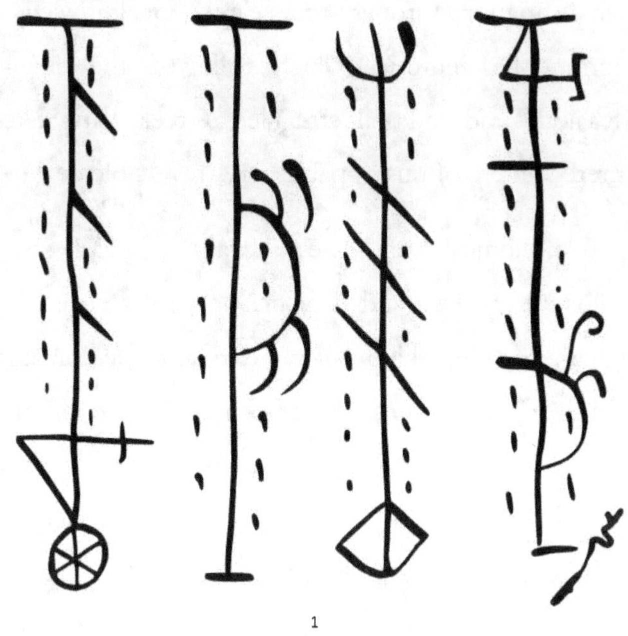

1

1 BETWEEN THREE ERAS

The Roman Republic, 167 BC

Greece was the cradle of ancient civilization and its philosophy represented the first man's project of

---

[1] *Galdrastafir* (magical staves) are sigils that were credited with supposed magical effect preserved in various Icelandic grimoires. This is a *Stafur gegn galdri,* a stave used against witchcraft.

transformation through the search for knowledge. During the centuries which followed the enemy invasions and internal struggles, Greek City-States entered an era of unstoppable and irreversible decline.

Apollonius of Crete was a Hellenistic philosopher. Tall and athletic he was a beautiful specimen of mankind with a dark complexion and slightly exotic features. His large, green eyes overhung a pasty, angular face. He was meticulous in everything he did. His hair was always cut to military length. Despite that, he was also very wise and a spiritual man. He came from an aristocratic family originally from Lycia, a mountainous territory of present-day Turkey, between the bays of Antalya and Fethiye. At the age of twenty, he moved to Athens, where he became a stoic scholar at the *Porch of Peisianax*, a philosophical school founded by Zeno of Citium, the founder of the Stoic school of philosophy.

In my opinion, Stoicism is still applicable today as a life approach, regardless of different religious, political or cultural views. Therefore, according to Stoic philosophy, the universe was governed by a law of reason; as a consequence, we can't avoid its inexorable force, but we can simply follow the law deliberately.

Apollonius was aware of living in an age of turbulent change, characterized by an interruption of the preestablished order due to internal conflicts and new political forces taking power. As a result of such instability, he fled from Athens and took refuge in Pella, an ancient city located in Central Macedonia, where he was employed as a private tutor to the son of Perseus, the last king of the Antigonid dynasty.

King Perseus, son of Philip V, tried in vain to rebuild the prestige of the Macedonian monarchy. Unfortunately, he did not 'realize' his mistake until it was too late: he underestimated the power of the Roman republic. His ambition could not be tolerated and it led to war with Rome.

The third Macedonian war, which took place between 171 BC and 168 BC, marked the end of his dynasty and the division of his kingdom into four client states to enfeeble it further.

Apollonius was taken prisoner by the Romans following these events. He was one who knew how to adapt to life and its sudden changes. He quickly realized that it would be important for his survival to be able to communicate with his enemies, so he quickly learned Latin.

His fellow inmate was called Polybius. He was Greek as well, but originally from Megalopolis, the capital of Arcadia. He was a historian and connoisseur of Roman culture. He could foresee the future through dreams, although he was unable to control this capacity. It was more like involuntary premonitions.

"I don't hate Romans, but I don't understand how it is possible to enslave other human beings."

"Come on my dear Polybius, I am sure that better days will come. You are a great man. I'm sure you will have the chance to prove your worth. Remember that while you are in this cell, you are always in a certain way free. Do you know what I mean?"

"I'm still free to think. Not even the arrogance of our enemies cannot make me stop thinking."

Apollonius was right. It was just a matter of time. The Roman consul Lucius Aemilius Paullus, the one who defeated Perseus in the decisive Battle of Pydna, noticed the talent of the two Greeks and required them as personal assistants and interpreters.

Paullus born into an illustrious Patrician family; its members held the highest offices of the state, from the early decades of the Republic to imperial times. After the victory of Pydna, as a gesture of acknowledgement, the Senate awarded him the nickname *Macedonicus*. Before becoming consul, he was an *augure*, a priest and official in the classical Roman world who had the task of interpreting the will of the gods by studying the flight of birds.

The 'augurs' were consulted whenever important decisions had to be made, both in times of war and in times of peace. Paullus was a member of the college of the 'augurs' until he assumed the role of *triumvir*[2] in 194 BC. He had a glorious *cursus honorum* ("ladder of offices")[3] behind him, characterized by a mixture of military and political administration posts.

---

[2] From Latin, it means "one of three men in the same office" or "of the same authority".

[3] It was the sequential order of public offices held by aspiring politicians in both the Roman Republic and the early Roman Empire. It was designed for men of senatorial rank.

4

Þingvellir, 15 August 1238

Eighteen years had passed since the beginning of
the "Age of the Sturlungs", a long period of violent

---

[4] This is a *Ægishjálmur*, a stave used to induce fear, protect
the warrior, and prevail in battle.

internal strife in mid-13th century Iceland. On a summer day in the year 1238, the Vikings gathered at Þingvellir, the so-called "Parliamentary Plains". This place is considered to be the oldest and longest-running parliament on Earth.

The *Althing* was an outdoor assembly of the Icelandic Commonwealth[5], where the country's most powerful leaders met once a year to promote new laws or to settle disputes. The island was at that time divided into four administrative quarters with a fixed number of thirty-nine lawmen.

One of the leaders participating in the peace meeting was Gissur Þorvaldsson, from the *Haukdælir* family clan. The name of his clan meant in Icelandic 'those of the Valley of the hawks'. King Haakon IV of Norway wanted to make Iceland his vassal. Many clans, including that of the *Haukdælir*, had become his supporters.

---

[5] It was the state existing in Iceland between the establishment of the Althing in 930 and the pledge of fealty to the Norwegian king with the Old Covenant in 1262.

Gissur was accompanied by Magnus Már Kristinsson, his bodyguard. This guy was also a kind of Viking shaman, but not exactly like a druid. He knew ancient Norse rituals and practiced healing spells. In most respects, there was nothing especially unusual in Magnus's physical appearance. It was his manner that most marked out the young warrior as unusual.

Gissur was allied with Kolbeinn the Young. He was the leader of the *Ásbirningar* a powerful family clan of well-known warriors and politicians. They lived in north-western Iceland and were the leading tribe of the Skagafjörður. Gissur and Kolbeinn were opposed by the *Sturlungar*, represented at the parliament by Sighvatur Sturluson and his son Sturla. This clan instead controlled the western and north-eastern part of the territory, and it was rich and influential.

Unluckily, the assembly was unsuccessful in bringing about peace. This time there was no way to find a peaceful solution to conclude that interminable conflict. As a consequence, the civil war culminated after a few days in the bloody battle of Örlygsstaðir, that came to be known by the largest Viking skirmish in Iceland's history.

6

Naples, February 2018

My name is Valentino Voto, research and cultural adviser at the Neapolitan University of Social Anthropology. A few months ago, I spent six months

---

[6] This is a *Angurgapi,* a stave carved on the ends of barrels to prevent leaking.

in Reykjavík to complete my thesis on the Norse mythology, and paranormal phenomena related to the soothsayers (*spámenn* in Icelandic) and the 'hidden creatures' (*Huldufólk*), the elves in Icelandic folklore.

The day before my departure to Iceland, I had a dream in which I experienced an incredible journey that I cannot explain rationally. I was already in Reykjavik. The memory of this experience was so vivid that when I woke up I thought I really had been there because the dream was so real.

One day I attended a seminar on the existence of parallel worlds and the use of past life regression. The event took place in Naples, my hometown in Italy.

The concept of a parallel dimension has been discussed for centuries by philosophers and anthropologists. This debate is largely unresolved and there seems to be no scientific explanation for it. Also, past life regression therapy has been strongly argued. Although the medical establishment does not support this practice, some physicians use hypnosis to take the patients back in time to trace and recover their unresolved conflicts.

Despite being a rational person (literally 'someone who is sensible and can make decisions based on intelligent thinking rather than on emotion'), I am utterly fascinated by these kinds of topics. It was on that occasion that I met my friend Marco for the first time.

"May I sit here?"

"Yes, go ahead," I replied politely.

There seemed to be a bond between us, as between old mates. We immediately had something in common. We were both linked to Iceland in some way.

"My name is Marco Oddur."

"I am Valentino. Do I understand correctly, your second name is Oddur? "

"My mother is from Reykjavík, I'm half Neapolitan, half Icelandic."

"What a coincidence! I just finished my Ph.D. in Anthropology at the University of Iceland."

Marco was a young man of rare beauty with raven hair and large dark eyes. He was blessed with a splendid graceful physique which had made him popular with the girls while attending college. He had joined a school of hospitality management, then after college, his career goals pulled him in different directions. He ended up graduating *cum laude* from University Federico II[7].

After completing his studies in biomedical engineering, my friend planned to leave Naples looking for job opportunities elsewhere. He knew one day he would be going away. That does not mean that he was not proud of his Neapolitan origins because, like me, he was.

Marco came from a rather unusual family. His father, Paolo Primativo, was a doctor originally from Avellino the ancient *Abellinum*, a center of the Samnite *Hirpini*. He was also a Boy Scout and a lover

---

[7] Founded by the emperor of the Holy Roman Empire Frederick II on 5 June 1224, it is the oldest public non-sectarian university in the world.

of mountains, very skilled both in rock and ice climbing techniques. During a trip to Iceland, he met his future wife, Helena Þóra. The two fell in love almost immediately; it seemed like love at first sight. It was the beginning of a long-distance relationship, but soon after they got married by a Lutheran pastor in Amalfi.

Birna, his maternal aunt, told him that it would not be difficult to find a job in Iceland as an engineer, so he decided to give it a try. Although he had never been there, he spoke Icelandic correctly. He bought a one-way ticket to Keflavik airport. He had never been more excited in his life.

After a half-hour wait, the seminar was finally starting. Unexpectedly they had to cancel the lecture on the existence of parallel worlds. At the time of this announcement, a psychotherapist next began lecturing on other topic. He explained to the audience that the purpose of regressive hypnosis was to stimulate memories of past traumatic events, and to eliminate them from the patient's mind.

To tell the truth, I was very curious about this controversial practice; in particular, I was interested in the possibility of being able to remember episodes referable to previous lives.

"I'd like to be hypnotized. Maybe I could get some answers on why I constantly have lucid dreams."

"I am an engineer and I remain a rational person, but I am also intrigued by inexplicable phenomena. That's why I am here today."

When Marco mentioned he was about to leave for Iceland, I confided to him that I felt a certain nostalgia for the time spent there. Meanwhile, our seminar was over and all the participants quickly left the classroom. However, we spent a few more minutes chatting with each other. I must admit that I had long thought about moving back to Reykjavík. Furthermore, the University of Iceland had offered me a one-year postdoc position in cultural anthropology. All those coincidences seemed to indicate my next destination.

"Marco, I was thinking that maybe we could travel together to Iceland. What do you think about it?"

"Come on, really? It would be wonderful to have you as a traveling companion. I'm leaving next week. If you write me your e-mail address, I will send you the details of my flight."

"Good idea, so we are sure to fly on the same plane."

Me and Marco greeted each other with a handshake, then I headed for the exit door. I was very happy to have met a new friend at this seminar.

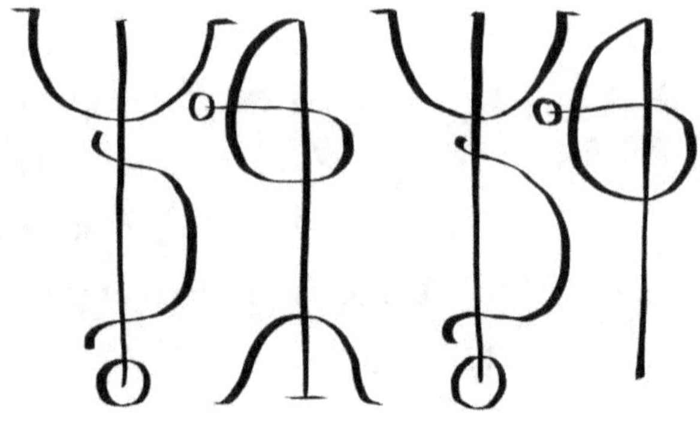

8

2 PREMONITIONS, DREAMS AND GHOSTS

Rome: the General's *domus*

Lucius Aemilius Paullus was a severe man and a loyal defender of ancient Roman tradition. At the end of the Third Macedonian War, he received the order from the Senate to pillaging Greek cities suspected of sympathizing with King Perseus cause. As a

---

[8] This is a *Draumstafir,* a stave used to dream of unfulfilled desires.

consequence, 70 villages were destroyed and 150,000 men were enslaved. Paullus returned with more than a thousand Achaean[9] hostages to Rome, including Apollonius and Polybius.

In reality, Paullus chose Apollonius not only to use him as a translator and educated servant, but he also had a more specific reason, based on what had happened during a propitiatory rite. One day, years before his military career, he was marking across the sky one imaginary line with his *lituus*[10]. The *Macedonicus* had a vision that he later connected with the Greek prisoner.

He felt like he was traveling toward an unknown destination. In this place, he saw little birds flying from angular rocks to the sky. He did not recognize the species. They had a black cap head, a face that was mainly white, and orange-red feet.

---

[9] Achaeans are the inhabitants of Achaea in Greece.

[10] A *lituus* was a particular stick used by *augurs* to mark out a ritual space.

Two strange men approached him in this distant and inhospitable land. They told him they were shipwrecked sailors, going to Thule Island. Later, one of them said that they were surrounded by a group of 'hidden people', a kind of supernatural beings that lived in nature. He warned him not to approach them himself, because only the 'Chosen One' could engage those creatures in a conversation.

The other shipwrecked man instead told him that an alliance with the *huldufólk*[11] could bring incredible power to Rome. He, therefore, again insisted that such a power would help the Republic to establish a millennial empire.

When Paullus awoke from the trance, he noticed some drawings on the ground. There was a chained wolf figure and also some words in ancient Greek:

Ἀπολλωνίδης

Θούλη

---

[11] The elves in Icelandic folklore.

The *Macedonicus* was sure this was a sign from the Gods that Apollonius was the 'Chosen One' mentioned in the prophecy of the shipwrecked man. Moreover, Thule was the name given to a legendary island. The Greek explorer Pytheas was the first to have written of this place, describing it as a land of fire and ice, characterized by unique atmospheric phenomena. In 330 BC, he set sail from Massalia[12] for an exploration of the Atlantic ocean.

In 167 BC, Lucius Aemilius Paullus obtained a triple triumph over three consecutive days. This was the peak of his career. Despite these accomplishments, the general was oddly unsatisfied. However, he did not forget this previous vision, which encouraged him to organize a new exploration to reveal the exact location of Thule and its secrets. He wanted to be remembered as the most devoted son of the Republic. The general wished to give to

---

[12] Now known as Marseilles, Massalia was a small city-state in the Greek Aegean Islands Founded in 517 B.C.

Rome such a power mentioned by the other castaway to establish a millennial empire.

His idea was to repeat Pytheas's journey, sailing exactly from Massalia, an independent Greek city-state and a faithful ally to Rome in the Second Punic War (218–201 BC). Thus, Apollonius and Polybius were summoned to meet the *Macedonicus* at his private *domus*[13]. They entered the main hall where the general was waiting for the two distinguished prisoners. After greeting them, he sat down and began to talk.

"I have an assignment for you. If you accept my proposal, you will be free to return to your own homes. But if you do not accept it, I guarantee that the rest of your life will be hard. Very hard."

The two Greeks were somewhat surprised by the general's words. They were happy but at the same time, they worried: what could he claim back for the promise of their freedom?

---

[13] It was the type of house occupied by the upper classes during the Republican and Imperial eras.

"My lord, we are very grateful and honored for the opportunity. What is it about?"

"Greeks are extraordinary sailors and your colonies were founded everywhere. I need you for an important mission on behalf of the people and the Senate of Rome. You will set sail from Massalia aboard a trireme[14]."

The general lied shamelessly. The Senate of Rome would never have authorized such an expedition into the unknown and based on a document, the fragments of the diary of Pytheas, absolutely unreliable.

"My lord, we are not sailors. Apollonius is a philosopher and I am a historian. We are just two ordinary men. We know nothing about navigation or how to establish a colony."

"Your past experiences and your intellectual capacities make both of you the right choice for this

---

[14] It was an ancient vessel and a type of galley that was used by the Phoenicians, ancient Greeks, and Romans.

mission. Apollonius, I'd like to nominate you as the ambassador of the Roman Republic to Thule. Polybius, you will be responsible for writing a journal of the voyage. You will have to reach the island of Thule, like the Greek navigator Pytheas did before."

"My lord, I know Pytheas's story, but I consider Thule a legend," replied Polybius.

"Well, then you will find out for yourself if it exists also in reality."

15

Örlygsstaðir, 21 August 1238

Magnus felt a profound sense of anguish that he could not control. Even though his faction retained a clear numerical superiority over the enemy, there was something inexplicable affecting him, corrupting his mind. Did it have something to do with the dream he had the night before the Battle of Örlygsstaðir? He had an alarming, even threatening nightmare. It was

---

[15] This is a *Deprún*, a stave used to kill an enemy's cattle.

an experience that shocked him. He was just watching from a spectator perspective what was happening in that dream.

Magnus remembered that he was standing next to a warrior. He did not recognize him. He was not a familiar face. That man was dressed in a complete suit of armor and carried strange equipment. He had a long curved oval body shield and a short sword. A moment later, another armed man appeared seemingly from out of nowhere. He seemed familiar, but Magnus couldn't place him. He was probably a Viking warrior. In his hand, he held a halberd while sitting on a huge chained wolf's back.

Magnus was just watching from a spectator perspective what was happening in front of him. Suddenly the beast made itself free from its chains, devoured the man who was sitting on its back and killed the other warrior with a throat bite.

An elf dressed in a black suit came together with other people in that gloomy place. Each of them carried an object, but apparently not a weapon. As soon as the wolf noticed Magnus's presence as a spectator, the beast's eyes began to burn like twin flames. Immediately after the wolf ran towards him. It took only a few seconds to reach Magnus. Then it attacked him with the greatest fury.

His fangs sank deep into the Icelander's neck. He screamed with agony, it was a bite strong enough to penetrate his armor and to tear through the skin. The wolf killed Magnus under the indifferent gaze of the elf and his companions.

He awoke from that terrifying nightmare. He had no doubts. The wolf was certainly Fenrir, a gigantic beast of Norse mythology; a dangerous creature, hungry and cunning at the same time, a symbol of chaos and destruction.

He interpreted that dream as a bad sign, even though he did not immediately understand the origin of that omen. More specifically, he felt a lack of balance around him. He sensed that something terrible would happen on the lowland plain of Örlygsstaðir. The question was, what exactly would happen to him?

The Sturlungar clan arrived at the battlefield first, followed by a thousand warriors. After a few minutes their allies reached Örlygsstaðir as well. Gissur and Kolbeinn had almost 1700 men in total[16]. Sighvatur and his son Sturla also came up in succession. When the two belligerents armies, facing each other, were positioned in the field, the war horn sounded and the battle began.

Magnus was close to Gissur. An attack came from behind. Magnus spun, bringing his shield up in the nick of time. His huge axe hummed through the air, catching the enemy warrior in the face. Then he struck the shield of another warrior, severed it in two, and badly wounded his arm. Finally, Magnus pointed his axe straight at the wounded enemy's heart, piercing his armor and killing him.

Both clans fought with such vehemence, vengeance and with no holds barred. Nevertheless, Gissur and his allies emerged victorious after a short battle. More than fifty warriors perished in that

---

[16] Karlsson, Gunnar (2000). The History of Iceland. pp. 80–81.

combat on the lowland plain of Örlygsstaðir, but almost all of them belonged to the *Sturlungar* clan. The *Haukdælir* clan only lost few men.

When Sighvatur and his son were disarmed, the rest of their companions quickly abandoned their positions and fled the battlefield in every direction.

"Damn traitors. Come back and fight! I am Sighvatur son of Sturla the Elder. I am a *goði*[17] and ruler of the *Sturlungar* clan. My family has always done the good of this island."

"Father, what will happen to us?"

"My son, we will die with honor. Only this matters now."

---

[17] It was a position of political and social prominence in the Icelandic Commonwealth. The term originally had a religious significance, referring to a pagan leader responsible for a religious structure and communal feasts, but the title is primarily known as a secular political title from medieval Iceland.

It wasn't like that. They did not die with dignity at all. That day there was an exception to the custom of guaranteeing the defeated enemy a dignified death.

They were made to kneel down with their heads lowered and were told not to look up. Then Gissur ordered Magnus to behead them with his ax. The first to be executed was Sturla. He was murdered immediately. His head rolled, leaving a trail of blood on the grass. Sturla probably did not even realize how he died.

"You just killed my son, but I'll take my revenge from the world of death. Always look behind you, because Fenrir will punish you. He will find you sooner or later," said his father.

Magnus was deeply affected by his words. He hesitated a few seconds before beheading Sighvatur. He was not happy to execute him, but he could not refuse his chief' order. Then he raised his ax again and, with all the strength, struck Sighvatur in the neck, cutting his head.

18

Naples: Before Leaving

Marco had already packed his bags. He would leave Naples the next day. He had a great desire to begin a new life in Iceland. His room was neat and tidy. There were a few posters on the walls, mostly football players, such as Diego Armando Maradona, one of the greatest of all time. A shelf was still packed with sports almanacs and Japanese manga: *Knights of the Zodiac* and *Fist of the North Star* were his favorite series.

Marco took a closer look at a physical map in a drawer: it was a map of Iceland. He started to fantasize, imagining he would find a good job in Reykjavík, worthy of his university studies, and even a loving girlfriend, someone with whom he could eventually create a family. Those were simply a young man' expectations. These positive thoughts gave him

---

[18] This is a *Valdemar's Protection Stave,* a stave used to increase favor and happiness.

the confidence to deal with the imminent change; so he decided he would not be worried, or overwhelmed by negative emotion and any of the challenges of his new life. Meanwhile, his mother entered the room.

"Have you finished packing your bags?"

"Almost."

"Marco *minn*[19], this house will feel so empty without you here. I'm going to miss you."

"I know mom, me too, but I will be just fine."

"I'm glad my sister Birna will host you until you and Valentino can find yourselves a place to stay."

"Mom you taught me how to speak your native language, but I don't think I know enough about our culture and traditions. For example, what do you know about ghosts and *Huldufólk*?"

---

[19] It means literally 'Marco mine'. The use of *mín* or *minn* after people's names, it is a way of expressing affection in the Icelandic language.

Helena burst into laughter and said, "why does this topic interest you? Weren't you the one who believes only in science?"

"This is correct, but I'm sure you have some interesting stories to tell. Valentino told me so many things about our folklore and legends that I suddenly became intrigued by them. He had a lot of psychic experiences, including dreams of future events."

"Dear Marco, I don't want to extinguish your enthusiasm, but Icelanders are particularly reserved and comfortable with their familiar routines. It won't be easy for you to feel like one of them, even if you already are half. They hardly make new friends with those who are outside their circle. Despite that, Iceland has always welcomed *útlendinga*[20] who contribute to our beautiful island."

"Hey, I didn't ask you for a sociological analysis of the society!" He said ironically.

----

[20] 'Foreigners' in Icelandic.

"I thought you were just kidding. All right then, I'll tell you about that time we had to contact a druid to bless grandma's house infested with evil entities."

Marco didn't regret asking, he was just a little surprised that his mother had a real paranormal experience during her teenage years. Thus Helena began her creepy tale.

"Grandma Solveig's house has two floors and a basement used as a small apartment for guests. It's quite a big house. In 1994 one of our relatives from Akureyri came to live in that basement. She was a student at the University of Reykjavík. In the beginning, there was no problem with her, but then something scary must have happened."

"What exactly happened? Did it have something to do with the basement?"

At that point, Marco was intrigued and wanted to know what happened next.

"I can't tell you exactly, perhaps the whole house. I remember that she left at night without telling us anything and drove straight back to Akureyri. When we entered through the internal door to the basement, her room was a mess. The drawers were all open. There were bits of old newspapers scattered everywhere around the floor. The small bathroom looked very dirty and the shower floor was covered with crumpled paper towels and scraps of toilet paper. It was an inexplicable and embarrassing situation, also because that girl had always been polite and kind to us."

"How did your family react to the situation? Did your cousin at least say she was sorry?"

"We were not angry with the girl. We never spoke again and I don't know what happened to her. However, my mother knew there was something wrong with our house. These paranormal phenomena worried her more than anything else. After that episode, she seemed alarmed and agitated by them, especially considering what your aunt has been through."

"Seriously Aunt Birna? What happened to her?"

It was time for Marco to go to sleep and rest for a while. The alarm clock was due to ring in just a few hours.

"Go to bed now. Maybe Birna will tell you in person her story some other time."

Marco was amused and excited by his mother's testimony. Her anecdote sounded to him like a horror movie.

"Goodnight Marco. I love you."

"Goodnight mom, *ég elska þig líka*[21]."

---

[21] "I love you too" in Icelandic.

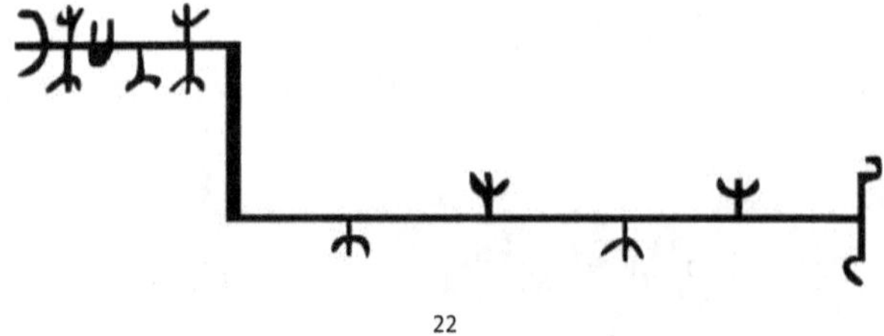

22

3 EVERYTHING FLOWS

First day: Departure from Massalia

Massalia was situated between white chalk cliffs and a turquoise crystalline sea, encircled by hills and grassy glades. At that time the Greek city-state was ruled by an aristocratic government and the power was in the hands of a small group of people. Its economy was indeed based on an intense mercantile activity, which made Massalia one of the major trading ports of the ancient world. As Apollonius slowly entered with Polybius through the city's gate, a fresh scent of lavender and thyme gave him new energy and hope.

---

[22] This is a *Feingur,* a fertility rune.

"Amazing, I had never seen such unspoiled vistas and beautiful landscapes," said Apollonius with a certain enthusiasm.

"To be honest I'm not interested in the scenic beauty of this place," said Polybius, concerned about their next trip.

"My friend, I understand your worries about Thule, I really do. But the only way out was to accept Paullus's proposal."

Finally, the Greeks arrived at their destination. When they reached the port area, Hipparchus of Nicaea welcomed them. The old man was a geographer and mathematician from the Bithynia region. He was considered to be the greatest ancient astronomical observer. Hipparchus was chosen by Paullus as a guide and cartographer on board. The astrologer was not a prisoner and not even a slave. He was a friend of the general. Paullus made his acquaintance in Rhodes when he was still holding the office of an *augur*. He was learning from Hipparchus his accurate mathematical models to explain the motion of the Sun and the Moon.

"Welcome to Massalia, dear brothers. I hope your trip here was a pleasant one. I am here at the explicit request of general Paullus to assist you on this journey."

Hipparchus explained to Apollonius and to his friend Polybius all he knew and was able to find out about Thule. While he was showing the route they were going to take, a group of men on horseback began to race toward them. They were all dressed in civilian clothes, but in reality, they were soldiers who had taken part in the battle of Pydna; veterans of the Third Macedonian War. One of them spoke to Apollonius.

"We have been ordered to escort you to Thule, and escort you to Thule we must."

The Greeks were stunned by the Roman efficiency in organizing that expedition. It was obvious that Paullus had spared no expense in providing them the best-trained men in every task. The whole crew consisted of more than two hundred people:

Apollonius of Crete, Polybius of Megalopolis and Hipparchus of Nicaea; six officers and a trierarch who commanded the trireme, named Protis of Massalia; twenty fully armed Roman legionaries, including Valerius Maximus, a trusted lieutenant of Paullus; 170 highly disciplined rowers, who provided the ship's motive power.

Short supplies of food and freshwater were taken aboard for the first few days of their long journey. Unfortunately, limited spaces did not allow the accumulation of large provisions. For this reason, numerous stops were planned until the last known port. Further north, everything would ultimately depend on their fate.

"I am aware of the risks of searching for Thule and I understand this is a voyage to an unknown destination. Pylibius, I also believe it will be the most incredible experience of our life."

"I see you're in a good mood, I'm glad for you Apollonius. But it would be irresponsible of me to expect that Thule does exist. I just hope for our survival."

"For me it exists," Hipparchus of Nicaea affirmed confidently, intruding on the conversation between the two compatriots, "it will take many days of navigation, but in the end, somehow, we will reach the island."

Meanwhile, the ship had set sail. A very handsome trireme named *Eos*[23], the Greek name of the goddess of dawn *Aurora* in Roman mythology. Despite Polybius's skepticism about Thule, the rest of the crew remained in good spirits and excited to participate in the expedition. Protis ordered his rowers to slow down just a little, so he could make a speech.

"The route to our destination will not be linear or even coherent. Maybe we'll get lost somewhere or maybe we'll need to go back to get food or water

---

[23] *Eos* was often described as being hope and rejuvenation to all living mortal beings as they woke up in the morning, filled with energy and ready to resume their work and journey and life in general.

supplies. I don't care if Thule exists or not at this point. What makes you feel alive? For me, what matters to us sailors is that we are now heading towards new horizons to explore. This must be enough to make us feel alive."

Protis's words put even the skeptic Polybius in a better mood. So he decided it was a good moment to begin writing the logbook requested by general Paullus. In truth, it was easy to find the right words to start it. He immediately recorded all the information available regarding the route they would follow. For him, the writing was not only an intellectual work but also a great tool to preserve a memory of past events. Thanks to his valuable testimony, Thule expedition could be remembered as a documented fact of history, written and personally verified.

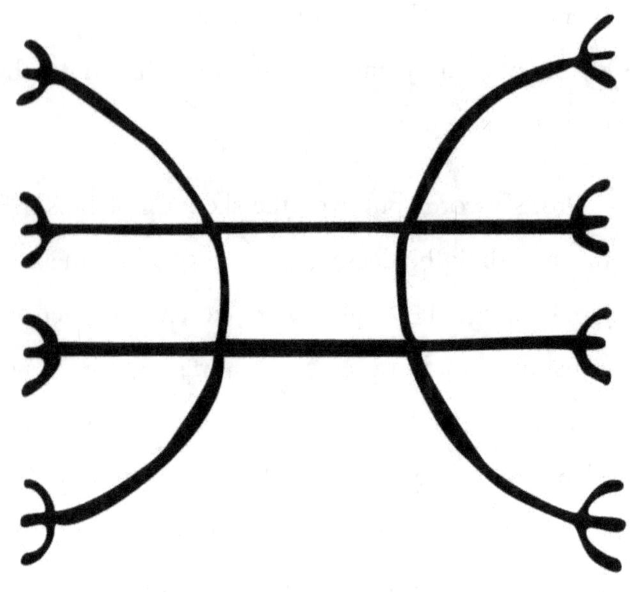

24

Örlygsstaðir: After the Battle

Magnus was still shocked and dumbfounded. It was unusual for him to lose control of himself, and

---

[24] This is a *Gapaldur*, is a stave to keep in the shoes, under the heel of the right foot, used to magically ensure victory in bouts of Icelandic wrestling (*glíma*).

being in a state of great agitation and anxiety. And, as he thought about the immediate aftermath of the battle of Örlygsstaðir, he became convinced that the huge wolf from his nightmares was in some way connected to the beheadings. He became afraid of being touched by a curse, as a sort of divine punishment for what he had done to Sighvatur and Sturla. If only he could go back in time and change things, he would without hesitation kill father and son on the battlefield. However, he felt dishonored for having murdered them that way.

He crept away from the combat zone without being noticed, his head hanging low as he walked alone in the dark. He walked three miles until he reached what he estimated to be a good, safe distance. Not too far down the path, something caught his eye, distracting Magnus from his dark thoughts. A strange rock aroused his curiosity. What caught his attention was the presence on his surface of mysterious symbols. These were symbols representing runes. Among these he readily recognized a magical stave. Magnus knew very well that whoever created it he had to be an expert sorcerer.

"I haven't seen anything like that in years," he said, speaking out loudly, "this sigil is used to invoke very evil spirits."

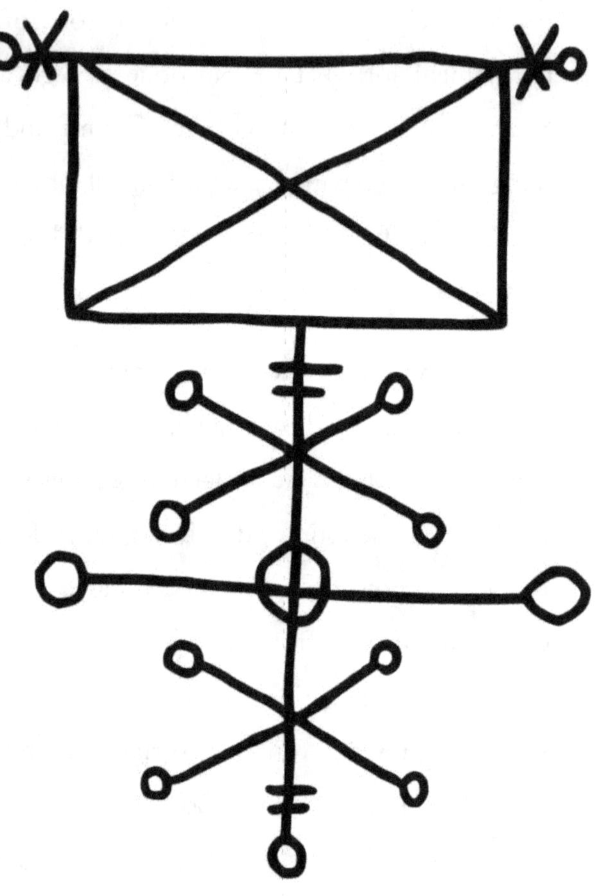

This sign was called in Icelandic: *Stafur til að vekja upp draug.* It was used to bring people back from death, to neutralize a ghost, and it also had the power to drive away evil spirits. According to an ancient book of magic, this symbol, to be effective, it must be carved on the skin of a horse's head with a mixture of blood from a seal, a fox, and a man. While Magnus was wondering who would draw such a thing in a remote and desolate place, someone was coming along the path toward him, holding a lantern.

"Why did you leave without saying a word? Can you explain or justify your behavior?"

Gissur was surprised to see Magnus there, looking so lost and confused. Something had upset him deeply, he realized. The atmosphere became black as midnight. Magnus had no intention of explaining himself. He looked at his chief, remained silent for a few seconds, then Gissur watched him enter a state of trance. Looking down to his chest, then pointing to it with both hands, he said in a strange guttural voice:

"Dear Gissur, I wonder if you know where you're going?"

Gissur was puzzled and did not know the reason for that question without apparent meaning.

" I don't understand you, are you okay?"

Magnus's eyes turned white. He began to move in a disjointed way, shaking like a damn thing. He drew strange geometric figures in the sky with his hands. Something evil had taken possession of his body. As if that wasn't enough, Gissur heard a dark and menacing growl coming from his shoulders. Unexpectedly his warrior pulled out his dagger and cut his throat. Gissur blinked his eyes a few times because he couldn't believe what he saw. It was a rapid and inexorable action. Within seconds Magnus slumped to the ground under the incredulous gaze of his master.

25

Naples, 28 February 2018

I decided to rely once more on my feeling and gut instinct rather than my rational thinking and logic.

---

[25] This is a *Ginfaxi*, is also a stave to keep in the shoes like the previous one, but under the toes of the left foot. It was used to magically ensure victory in bouts of Icelandic wrestling (*glíma*).

I heard a voice inside telling me to change my life. It encouraged me to step out of my comfort zone. Somehow I knew my new mindset would soon prove to me that I could face any challenge. Iceland was calling.

Honestly speaking, I could not rationally explain this nostalgia for *Garðarshólmi*[26]. I had often the sensation that its landscapes, with deep contrasting colors, had stolen my soul. Despite that, no matter what, Naples would always be my "safe haven place", where I was born and raised, surrounded by the love of my father Antonio, my mother Anna and my brother Massimo.

"Valentino, I don't understand the reason why you are leaving us again. Why would you want to move to the North Pole? Stay with us a little longer. Aren't you happy here?" My father Antonio asked,

---

[26] There are numerous different names for Iceland, which have over the years appeared in poetry or literature. This one means "Island of Garðar". Garðar Svavarsson was the first Norseman to sail around Iceland.

with a certain sadness.

Iceland was for him and my mother the North Pole, just a cold and inhospitable land. They couldn't understand the decision that I made. My mother even tried to find a justification for it. She was convinced that I was in love with some local girl from Reykjavík.

"There are so many good and beautiful girls around. Why can't you find a girlfriend in Naples?"

"Mom, I'm not interested in that kind of thing. At least not at this moment in time. I simply need to complete my studies, that's all."

I was lying somehow because I was still hoping that Gudrun, my Platonic love, could exist also in reality. She was probably just an Icelandic lady my imagination created, but sometimes I felt like she was real and not just a dream. Besides that, I was obsessed with old Norse traditions and sagas that I had previously documented for my doctoral thesis; in particular, I was interested in ghosts and elves stories.

Father Santoro was worried about my interest in

such topics. He was an old Jesuit priest who had become my friend and confidant. He considered them harmful and detrimental to my soul. To tell the truth, I frequently had premonitions about everyday little things. I found them scary sometimes. One day Father Santoro told me that Earth is populated by demons and unclean spirits.

"Valentino, unfortunately, they are everywhere. We priests and exorcists are not always able to save souls. Evil spirits are dangerous and they hate human beings. You must be careful to investigate whatever is hidden in the darkness."

His words were certainly not encouraging for my research, but I wanted to investigate further. When I started studying occultism, it seemed unlikely that this great spread of irrational ideas could only be the fruit of superstitions and popular ignorance. I always thought there was something bigger. I was fascinated by these stories.

Marco's father came to pick me up with his convertible car. My brother Massimo made a request before I passed out of the door.

"This time don't forget to bring me a shark's tooth necklace. You should also have one, it will protect you from the dangers."

Massimo was younger than I. He was diagnosed with autism spectrum disorder when he was three years old. I never had a problem with that. I looked at him as having a creative brain, which means his brain works differently than mine. Despite that, he had a completely normal existence: he loved to draw, to collect beer bottles and to follow S.S.C. Napoli, his favorite Italian professional football club. After greeting him and my parents, I went outside and seated myself in the car with Marco. Our Iceland adventure had officially begun.

"The day we've been waiting for has finally come!" Marco said excitedly.

As we arrived at the airport Paolo hugged his son and said, "have a wonderful trip, I love you."

"Can I have another hug dad?"

"You can have as many hugs as you want!"

I also said goodbye to Paolo; then we turned our back and headed towards the terminal. It was going to be a very long journey with a five-hour stopover in Berlin. While we waited for our next flight, I spent some time thinking about the meaning of friendship. Friendship is that 'unexpected gift' that you receive when you least expect it. For this reason, it would never be reasonable to be disappointed with old fellows with whom you no longer have contact.

Old friends had disappeared from my life: who had married, who had other interests different from mine, or who had simply forgotten me. Nevertheless, I could not blame them. I felt no resentment against Gianni, Alessandrone, Luca and all the other guys from my high school period. I had realized that whoever had disappeared, sooner or later, would be replaced by new friends, more suited to my new social expectations in everyday life. I believe this happens all the time because as individuals we are constantly learning and we are also constantly evolving. As Heraclitus of Ephesus said: "everything flows" (πάντα ῥεῖ), and consequently nothing is permanent, because we are continually shaped by the vicissitudes of life and all the accumulated experiences.

That's why I came to the conclusion that Marco Oddur Primativo was exactly that "unexpected gift".

27

4 *PAVOR NOCTURNUS*

Third day: Arrival at the Port of Malaca

The *Eos* had arrived in Malaca[28], another Greek
city-state, which was taken, as Massalia, under the

---

[27] This is a *Hólastafur,* a stave used to open hills.

protective wing of the Roman Republic. It was the last stop in friendly territory. Most of the crew were resting and those that were awake were helping with the supply operations. But unfortunately for them, sleeping on the deck was not as comfortable as sleeping on land or in a real bed.

Polybius was also tired. Despite the discomfort of being onboard a trireme, he immediately fell into a deep sleep; and as soon as sleep came, his terrible nightmares visited him again. He had a recurring dream of men torturing him to death. The dream was always the same. The place seemed more like a dark parallel world, where his death occurred because of the wounds inflicted by several torturers. This was a disquieting experience, during which he could not even distinguish reality from imagination. Polybius

---

[28] Malaca was the Latin name of Malaga, now city and port of Spain. The romanization of Malaca was carried out peacefully through a *foedus aequum*, a treaty recognizing both parties as equals, obligated to assist each other in defensive wars or when otherwise summoned.

would wake up screaming in pain, perceiving himself as having no control over his own body.

That night, however, he had a similar dream but from another perspective. He saw someone else tortured and executed by a group of soldiers. This time he was just a spectator. Suddenly, this man was beheaded and his body fed to a huge chained wolf. While Polybius was watching the scene from above, the beast noticed him. The wolf looked straight into his eyes, and then said these words:

"Thule will be your grave if you continue this journey. You must be careful to investigate whatever is hidden in the darkness. The Romans are demons, and they will be defeated one day."

At that point, Polybius woke up trembling. He had his mind darkened by an imaginary pain. His face was damp with sweat and he was unable to breathe regularly. He could not stop thinking about the wolf's enigmatic words. Was the dream a premonition, or just the result of a stressing period?

Surely a premonition, he thought. Polybius was convinced that he was being abandoned to his fate because searching for Thule would be a fatal undertaking.

29

Haugsnes peninsula, 19 April 1246

Haugsnesbardagi is said to be the bloodiest battle ever fought on Icelandic soil, with about 110 casualties in total.

---

[29] This is a *Kaupaloki*, a stave used to prosper in trade and business.

Eight years had passed since the victory over the *Sturlungar* clan at Örlygsstaðir and Magnus's mysterious suicide. This time, however, the outcome was not favorable to Gissur Þorvaldsson. On that occasion, his clan was defeated by the forces loyal to Þórður Sighvatsson. He was the son of Sighvatur Sturluson and the brother of Sturla Sighvatsson, both killed in the Battle of Örlygsstaðir. Following these events, Þórður travelled around Iceland, gathering enough forces to revenge his family.

Gissur was surrounded by the enemy. The attacks were coming from all sides. He was slightly wounded in the head. Many of his men were killed during fierce hand-to-hand combat. He heard screams coming from all directions. *Sturlungar* casualties were everywhere scattered over the battlefield. Despite the desperate situation, Gissur continued to fight hard, holding his shield high and brandishing his halberd.

"Where are you Magnus son of Kristinn? Today I am alone in facing the Sturlungs without your mighty ax. I not only lost my bravest warrior but a true friend as well. May the gods protect you, may the gods help me."

Unfortunately, this time Odin and the other deities were not on his side. Þórður was victorious.

"Tell your people to lay down their weapons. If they don't lay down their swords and axes, I will order my men to exterminate all of you," Þórður said in a persuasive voice.

Gissur forced himself to obey his request. He realized there was no chance of victory and no way of fighting back. In the end, they all surrendered, and no other lives were taken. The Battle of Haugsnes marked the end of the *Haukdælir* clan's exclusive hegemony in Iceland. Despite that, Gissur was inexplicably spared.

"Even if you murdered my father and my brother, I am not going to execute you. I won't be a coward like you!"

Gissur did not react to his words. There was resignation on his face. It was clear that there was nothing more to be done. Then he ordered his men to retreat from the battlefield. It was a painful defeat, which, however, did not compromise the existence of his clan.

"I am forced to admit defeat, but it's good to know we fought. We did not run away from the battleground. It's true, we lost this battle, but we are not losers. Our strength doesn't always come from a victory. It also comes from struggles and hardship. Everything that we went through today, it will prepare us for the next fight."

Slowly, for the sake of the wounded, Gissur and his warriors left Haugsnes. They kept on walking without stopping for 5 miles until they found a good spot to set up camp for the night. This place did not look exactly hospitable. It was an uninhabitable volcanic desert, which was characterized by mountain blocks of igneous and metamorphic rocks. All of a sudden a lady came out of nowhere. As she approached the group of men, a spooky atmosphere pervaded the whole camp. Her eyes looked inhuman, and Gissur felt instantly alarmed.

She knew who he was. She had long white hair that she kept in braids, wrapped around her head like a crown. Her skin was very white. Her name was Thordis. She looked deep into his eyes, claiming to possess the gift of foresight. Then she moved very close to him and put her left hand on his forehead. It was at this moment she started hissing some sort of spell.

Now let's see if you understand this.

Why the sun and the moon live in the sky?

The foolish men are always anxious for justice.

A monstrous wolf will rise against you.

Traitor, exterminator.

Who will save you now?

No one is coming to save you.

Inexplicably, all his men fell into a deep sleep, hitting the ground like sacks of potatoes. Also, Gissur fainted shortly after. His face had an expression of fear; it was as if something terrifying was happening right in front of his eyes. Meanwhile, the shadows of the night had had entirely enveloped the lava desert.

30

Reykjavík, 3 May 2018

We landed at Keflavík airport in the middle of the afternoon. I must admit that thanks to an interesting book and a great harmony between me and Marco, this journey was pleasant. Despite

---

[30] This is a *Lukkustafir*, a stave used to open a lock without a key.

horrible weather conditions, characterized by heavy rainfall and strong winds, our arrival in Iceland was like a dream coming true. We took the bus heading to the city center, almost one hour away from the airport.

Marco's aunt came to pick us up at the station. Birna was a pretty middle-aged woman with blonde hair and striking good looks. She spoke very well Italian, which I could easily understand. In high school, she took Italian classes but never really became fluent until she went to *Belpaese*[31] several times. She offered a room in her home for me and Marco to stay until we could find a place of our own. The elderly grandmother was also living in her big apartment. *Amma*[32] Solveig had recently moved in with her daughter due to a fall that she suffered at her huge villa in *Suðurgata*.

---

[31] This is the classical poetical appellative for Italy, meaning the "beautiful country" in Italian, due to its mild weather, cultural heritage and natural endowment.

[32] It means "grandmother" in Icelandic.

During the flight, Marco had told me everything about some ghostly phenomena which happened there. I couldn't wait to hear the rest of the story from his aunt. What I found intriguing, was the fact that I could refine and extend my studies of Norse mythology and paranormal phenomena with new experiences and connections. When we arrived at Birna's house in *Vesturbær*, I immediately met *amma* Solveig. His grandmother spoke only Icelandic, so Marco acted as my interpreter. Solveig was an elderly lady in her eighties, sprightly and full of life.

"I and my mother want to welcome you guys. It is a great pleasure to have you here. I would like to take this opportunity also to brush up my Italian."

"Thank you Birna for the warm welcome and also for your hospitality. We will try to find accommodation as soon as something opens up."

"Sure not a problem, like I said no rush, take your time. We've already prepared dinner for this evening. I made just for you a fermented shark, called *hákarl*, and sour ram's testicles. They are national dishes of Iceland," Birna said, trying very hard to remain serious.

"I am sure they'll be delicious!" I replied, winking my eye at her.

"I'm just kidding Marco. I wish you could've seen your expression, though. It was priceless. I made a lasagna *Alla Birna*, and also a delicious Icelandic lamb with potatoes and carrots."

Solveig was enchanted by his Italian grandson. She was delighted to see him again after three years since the last time she was in Naples. She used to travel a lot. Before her accident, Solveig had been a very active woman. She loved working in her garden during the summer. The old lady was so proud of herself when her house was surrounded by plants and flowers, that she had planted there.

"*Amma* had a bad experience in *Suðurgata*'s villa. She believes that someone pushed her from behind. Furthermore, she thinks there are evil spirits in her home. Do you guys believe in ghosts?"

"Birna, I believe these things are true. I would like to spend some time there for my studies. I too witnessed some unexplainable phenomena in the last years," I told her.

"We still own the house, but we are trying to sell it. You and Marco are welcome to spend one sleepless night there, but know, once you go, you are on your own, you need to be aware and not take stupid risks," she replied mysteriously.

Solveig interrupted our conversation. From the kitchen, she motioned for Birna to come. She seemed rather annoyed at something. An then I thought she must have realized that we were talking about ghosts, although she didn't understand Italian. Half an hour later, dinner was ready; the dining table was strangely laid for five people, and a blanket with a floral theme was placed on a stool, which was next to me.

"Are we waiting for guests?"

"Not really, great-grandmother Saga is already here."

"Who? Didn't she died fifty years ago?" Marco asked, surprised.

"You are right. This one is still her favorite chair, we always keep a seat for her."

I didn't understand if Birna was just kidding us, or if it was an Icelandic tradition to keep a place for a dead relative on certain occasions. Then, when Solveig retired to her room, Birna wanted to satisfy our curiosity regarding the paranormal phenomena she experienced first-hand in that house.

"I will tell you about my personal experience. Mamma *mín* is still obsessed with the episodes that have occurred in these years at *Villa Gudrun*. So I preferred not to talk about it before when she was still here."

When I heard that name I jumped out of the chair. As I mentioned earlier, I had a strange dream that I might have confused with reality, or I thought so.

In that dream, I was walking towards Spaccanapoli (literally 'split Naples'), an east-west-oriented road, called

Decumanus Maximus. Then quite unexpectedly, I was surprised by a young lady. I thought maybe she was a tourist asking for directions. Her eyes were magnetic, of a gray-green color. She looked like a familiar face, though I was sure I did not know her. She approached me, and I was surprised by her elegant ways to speak.

"Hello Valentino, I am Gudrun," she said in a perfect Italian accent.

She was incredibly beautiful. She wore vintage jeans and a sweater that had bizarre and geometric designs. Then she started to tell me how the members of a sect of intellectuals, philosophers and bankers would have the ability to contact the hidden creatures to obtain earthly benefits.

"Draumfarir tíðar, mun hurðum upp ljúka[33]," she repeated this sentence two or three times, before vanishing into thin air.

"Is everything okay?" Marco asked, looking at me in awe.

---

[33] "Vivid dreams will eventually open gates", this was the meaning.

"Yes, of course. I'm just a little tired, that's all."

"Valentino, how suggestible are you?" Birna enquired.

"Not at all," I reassured her.

I think she knew I was lying somehow. There have been so many strange things happening to me since I met Gudrun in my vivid dreams. That's exactly why I have great respect for the supernatural world and the 'unseen'. However, as soon as we sat down, Birna started telling us her story.

"When I was about thirteen years old, I was diagnosed with night terrors disorder, also known as *pavor nocturnus*. It caused me to have terrible nightmares, sleepwalking, and hallucinations. My bedroom was next to Helena's room. One night I woke up screaming, calling your mother for help. It was an irrational reaction, but by the time she'd entered my bedroom, I was incredibly agitated and in an altered state. She was very patient and helped me calm down. Then we went to the bathroom together. When Helena was outside waiting for me, I saw a spooky figure reflected in the mirror. It was a body without its head. I screamed like a madwoman. Although your mother had not seen anything, she started screaming too."

Glued to our chairs, me and Marco listened to her story with trepidation. I must admit I was so shocked to hear these things. It seemed to me she had a great accuracy to recall these events. Birna continued her story, stopping every time as I and Marco interrupted her with questions.

"Did it happen other times?"

"Yes, quite often. Your grandmother used to say that I should be afraid of the living, not of the dead. Despite her reassurance, it was scary to see ghosts both at home and on the street."

"Mom never told me anything about your problem," her nephew said surprised.

"I'm sorry for what you had to go through. Has anyone helped you?" I asked her.

"Yes, a Japanese lady who lived in Reykjavík at that time. Her name was Sakura. We contacted her and she was happy to perform a purifying ritual. This was a great relief. That woman was into shamanism. She had to close a canal that I had inadvertently opened with the afterlife. I am grateful to Sakura because thanks to her I got my life back."

"Well if we won't sleep tonight, I know who I should blame," Marco said, trying to break the tension that had arisen.

After a few minutes of silence, Birna said goodnight and retired to her bedroom. Her story was the most shocking I had ever heard from an Icelander.

The two of us remained alone in the kitchen for an hour. We were both absorbed in our thoughts. From time to time we exchanged jokes, perhaps to ease the tension created by Birna's story. However, the temptation to talk about it was too strong and I asked the first question.

"What idea did you get?"

"My aunt is a reliable person. I know her well and I believe that the episodes she told us tonight really happened."

"I was baffled. Who knows, maybe they are real, but at the same time they could also be explained rationally."

"Of course, I agree with you, Marco. That's why I would like to spend some time in that house, also to understand if it is a place where the mind can be influenced."

In the meantime, I sent a message to my father Antonio to let him know that our journey had gone quite well and we had arrived at our destination. Marco did the same. In the end, we drank a cup of chamomile tea, after which we decided to go to sleep. Our day was finally over.

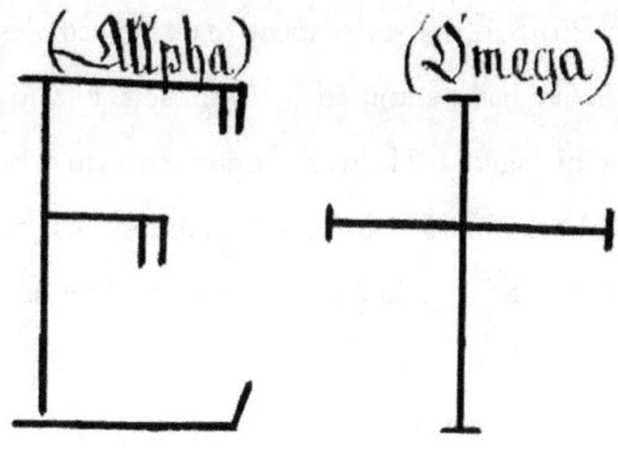

34

5 THE WORLD UP AND DOWN

Eighth day: Atlantic Ocean

A full moon lit up the landscape almost like daylight. Meanwhile, the trireme was at the mercy of the waves. Seven sailors had fallen into the sea due to strong winds. The situation on board was critical and the crew's morale had dropped considerably. Many

---

[34] This is a *Lukkustafir*, whoever carries this symbol with them encounters no evil, neither on the sea nor on the land.

believed that that journey, in search of a legendary and perhaps non-existent island, was cursed. Even Captain Protis began to suspect that, nevertheless he would never have admitted it to himself, let alone in front of his sailors. He was a brave and duty-bound man, so he would go all the way. Apollonius, on the other hand, did not know what to do. The state of things seemed complex and complicated to solve with one of his philosophical ideas. Not being an expert in navigation and marine currents, he did not feel like giving any advice to the captain. He was aware that the search for the island of Thule could lead them from one moment to another to a tragic end.

"The sea is stormy and we are prisoners of a destiny that we have not chosen," Polybius said concerned.

"Come on, I'm sure we'll somehow save ourselves. We must pray Poseidon so that the storm ends soon and hope that the ship does not sink in the meantime," replied Apollonius, feigning optimism and devotion to the god of the sea.

Hipparchus of Nicaea tried desperately to keep his balance and to resist the impact of the waves on the trireme. He was the first to use the grading grid, to determine geographic latitude from star observations, and not only from the Sun's altitude, and to suggest that geographic longitude could be determined using of simultaneous observations of lunar eclipses in distant places. With his solar and lunar theories and his trigonometry, he may have been the first to develop a reliable method to predict solar eclipses. Despite his great scientific success, Hipparchus was an elderly person and he was so exhausted he could barely stand.

"For Zeus, Poseidon and Apollo's sake! Who will save us now? "

"I know that only the god of the dead and the king of the underworld, the ruthless Hades, will hear your stupid prayers," Polybius said sarcastically.

Although the situation was tragic, the Roman soldiers were the only ones to remain calm. Their commander, Valerius Maximus Galba, belonged to Paullus's old guard. He had fought for the *Macedonicus* in the wars against the Lusitanians, the Ligurian pirates and of course the last Macedonian king. His face showed no emotion. Then, turning to Apollonius, he exclaimed:

"I promised to General Paullus that I would protect you and escort you to Thule. You will return home, be sure of it. You will not die today."

His words were not random. Valerius Maximus was convinced of what he had just said. However, Poseidon was not yet willing to calm the ocean. Indeed the storm became increasingly violent. Thus the trireme began to deviate due to the powerful marine currents.

The captain and his sailors were no longer able to control the ship. Now that storm had become furious. As a result, terror and confusion reigned supreme from bow to stern: there were those who wept desperately and those who sought divine assistance from their gods. Protis, in spite of everything, encouraged his men and invited them not to give up.

At a certain point, the trireme suffered an apparently irreparable and at least inexplicable damage. Something or someone had caused a huge gash on the left side of the ship, allowing the seawater to penetrate inexorably into the hull within seconds. Apollonius was always watched over by the Roman guards. Polybius and Hipparchus, on the other hand, embraced each other and tried not to be sucked into the ocean.

"Every man for himself!" A sailor yelled.

Onboard a general panic ensued, while the darkness of the night had taken over the light of the full moon. The world of Apollonius was now upside down.

35

The Black Mine: The Other Dimension

Gissur was stunned, shocked and disoriented as he thought he had died during the battle of Haugsnes, where he came across the force of Þórður Sighvatsson. He made an effort to remember what

---

[35] This is a *Máladeilan,* a stave used to win in court.

had happened. He recalled being spared by Þórður at the end of that fratricidal battle between *Sturlungar* and *Ásbirningar*. Nevertheless, Gissur was still having difficulty remembering events occurred after the retreat from the battlefield.

His soul had travelled rapidly across an astral corridor, and then returned in his material body. He has unexpectedly arrived into another dimension. It was a dark place, where time perception slowed all around him; a place where the sins of the past no longer mattered.

He kept on walking into the darkness with no precise destination in mind as though he was trying to lose some tail. At a certain point, he arrived under the walls of what appeared to be an underground village. Waiting for him in front of a stone gate was a strange creature dressed in black. At first sight, it seemed similar to a human being, although it was rather short in stature.

"Welcome, Gissur, and thank you for coming here. I see that you finally managed to open the portal."

"Who are you? Where am I?"

"My name is Malachy and I am the leader of the *Døkkálfar*[36]. This is the Black Mine, the point of contact with the afterlife. We, the dark elves, are the guardians of the subsoil and the rocks. You're one of Malachy's chosen people."

"The chosen what?"

"You will be made aware of what you need to know at the right time. Luckily you somehow managed to open the portal!"

"What the Hell is this portal? Tell me what I'm doing here and what you want from me!"

"Everything has its own time. Yours is not finished yet."

---

[36] In Norse mythology, *Dökkálfar* ("Dark Elves") and *Ljósálfar* ("Light Elves") are two contrasting types of elves. The Dark Elves and the Light Elves are attested in the Prose Edda, written in the 13th century by Snorri Sturluson.

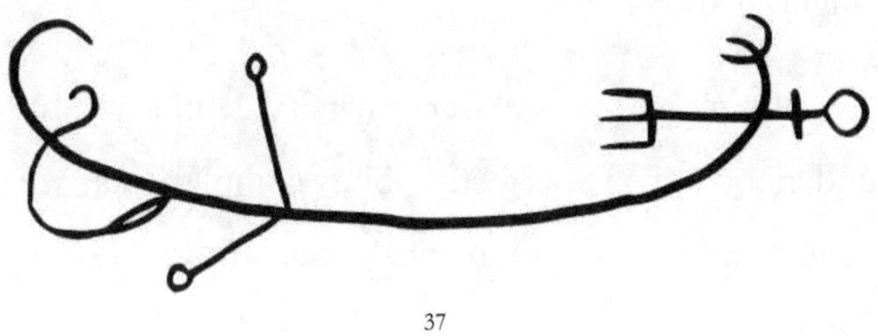

37

Reykjavík, 4 May 2018 (morning)

When we woke up in the morning at Birna's home, we were rested and regenerated as if we had spent the whole night in a wellness center. Breakfast was a pleasant surprise for me. Grandmother Solveig had prepared thin pancakes called *pönnukökur*, and decorated with kiwi, strawberries, and cream.

"Maybe something got lost in the translation. Please Birna, could you tell your mother that these pancakes are delicious? I spoke to her in Icelandic, but I'm not sure she understood me," I told her,

---

[37] This is a *Skelkunarstafur,* a stave used to make your enemies afraid.

trying to avoid looking foolish because of my poor language knowledge.

"Don't worry about that Valentino. Mum understood you perfectly. She compliments you, saying that you will soon speak Icelandic like Halldór Laxness[38]!"

The atmosphere was so euphoric that we felt so revved up to be there. We decided that we would spend the second night in the "haunted" house. We were unconsciously determined to investigate those alleged paranormal phenomena. I realized that the villa was in *Suðurgata*, the same street where my Ecuadorian friend Felix had lived before. It was a street west of the city center of Reykjavík, a stone's throw from Hólavallagarður Cemetery, a calm and peaceful site with dense trees and redwings which come within a meter.

---

[38] He was an Icelandic writer. He won the 1955 Nobel Prize in Literature; he is the only Icelandic Nobel laureate.

I began to tell Marco a little about my doctoral thesis, in which I tried to give my interpretation to some bizarre episodes that had happened to me. Such situations had perhaps over-stimulated my imagination and fueled nostalgia for this Arctic country. For this reason, I had imagined suffering from a singular pathology, a state of psychological dependence that I called "Iceland Syndrome". It is a condition which caused me to develop obsessive ideas, delusions or other psychosis-like experiences that are triggered by a visit to this island.

The earth is still forming here, due to the intense activity that takes place in its subsoil. Perhaps in the past, the Icelanders have begun to turn to the supernatural, finding no explanation for the natural phenomena to which their lovely island is constantly subjected. These phenomena can likely be explained by the scientific method, therefore only after more information has been acquired.

Marco was interested in my theories. I had elaborated them thanks to the precious material provided during my Ph.D. by my supervisor,

Professor Jón Magnusson, a world-famous anthropologist and an expert in runes, the old alphabet used by the ancient Germanic peoples.

"Have you ever heard of the *Gissur's pact*?" Marco said, interrupting my story.

"What is it?"

"Gissur Thorvaldsson was the *goði* of the Haukdælir clan."

"I know the meaning of this word. The *goði* was a priest. Jón explained to me that this Norse term was often engraved on the rune stones found in Denmark and Sweden."

"Precisely. In this case, it indicates the fact that Gissur was the lord of his territory of origin and not a priest."

"*Bravo* Marco! I see that your knowledge is greater than mine in this field. Why did you mention this pact?"

"Gissur made an agreement with King Haakon IV to make Iceland a vassal of the Norwegian crown.

The king assured him in return that he alone would be his political referent on the island. According to a Norse legend, there would have been another pact, but with an evil entity instead. Thanks to the help of an elf, Gissur became the unique leader of all the Icelandic clans. In return, however, it had to overcome a very dangerous test of courage."

"I know the figure of Gissur Thorvaldsson, but I didn't know about this story," I admitted.

Despite his explanation, it seemed strange to me that Marco was interested in this pact and that he needed to talk to me about it. I could not find a logical connection with our chat. After walking for about twenty minutes we arrived in *Suðurgata*. A young woman promptly caught our attention. She seemed to be waiting for us. When he saw us coming, he came towards us.

"Hi Marco, I am your cousin Gudrun. And you must be Valentino, right?" She spoke with a perfect Italian accent.

"Hello. You must excuse me, but I don't have cousins, maybe you mistake me for someone else," Marco answered with some embarrassment.

I felt my heartbeat rise. Surprisingly, Gudrun was identical to the girl I had dreamed (or met?) in Naples. Maybe my mind was playing tricks on me. On the other hand, it seems that 'Déjà vu' is caused precisely by an abnormality of the brain. It was not the first time that happened to me, but she was so real. As it had already happened, I was probably overlapping the past with the present in my imagination.

"Indeed we are not directly cousins, but being half Icelandic, I assume that at some point in the past your ancestors were related to mine."

This may seem unlikely, but legends claim that Icelanders all roughly share the same family tree, as all descendants of an Icelandic Roman Catholic bishop and poet, called Jón Arason. He fathered numerous children. However, this anecdote did not explain why she knew our names.

Who was that Icelandic girl who spoke perfect Italian?

39

6 THE PACT

Tenth day: Crossing the Unknown Sea

Valerius Maximus had made a pact with General Paullus: Apollonius had to survive at all costs. Despite the damage caused by the storms and the missing sailors, fortunately, the trireme had not sunk.

---

[39] This is a *Rosahringur minni,* a stave used for a lesser circle of protection.

However, although the forces of nature had put a strain on the promise made to Paullus, the Roman soldier and his men had best repaired the great gash in the side of the ship. After all, the Romans were formidable soldiers. As they prepared for this mission, they were to preference in their minds that they will never give up. They were trained to resist until the end of the journey.

"What you have done is incredible, a prodigy. You have saved *Eos*. I will be grateful to you forever," said Protis, visibly moved.

"If I were you, captain, I would worry about finding as soon as possible a port to dock and stock up on food and provisions. Otherwise tomorrow, or at most the day after tomorrow, we will all sentenced to death," replied Valerius Maximus scornfully.

He had a right to be alarmed. Indeed, they weren't out of danger at all. There was nothing good about what has happened the previous night. And there was certainly nothing to celebrate. Valerius Maximus knew that the trireme was venturing into unknown waters. The strong winds had caused the crew to lose their bearings. Furthermore, food and water supplies were increasingly scarce.

"I feel guilty. I have to admit we got lost. I am afraid that I will be severely punished for my mistake. If my calculations were correct, we should be close to the *Cassiterides* islands. Given the current situation, I have no idea where we are," Hipparchus admitted heartily.

The *Cassiterides* were an ancient geographical name of islands, situated somewhere near the west coasts of Europe. The Greek historian Herodotus had only vaguely heard of them, "*from which we are said to have our tin,*" but did not discount the islands as legendary. At a time when geographical knowledge of the West was still scanty, the voyage of Pytheas of Massalia was a particularly notable example of a very long voyage.

In the classical age, sailors made use of several techniques to determine their location, including the understanding of the winds and their tendencies. By the third century BC, the Greeks had begun to navigate following the stars, in particular, they used as a reference point the Little Bear, *Ursa Minor*. The stars, however, had inexplicably disappeared from the sky, rendering vain Hipparchus's calculations.

"You have not made any mistakes in truth, and you certainly do not deserve a punishment of any sort. Now more than ever, we are all victims of a destiny that we have not chosen. We are just puppets in the hands of the gods," replied Apollonius.

"I provided Captain Protis with the best route to follow. I based my calculations on both the motion of the stars, as well as the indications of Pytheas and the Phoenician sailors. Unfortunately, that damn storm has upset all my plans. And then, where did my stars go?"

Their conversation was abruptly interrupted by an exceptional event that triggered the panic on board again. In truth, everyone was terrified and speechless. The following events followed one another in rapid succession. A large sea monster had emerged from the depths of the ocean.

"I am the *Miðgarðr*[40] snake, the most powerful demonic and ruthless sea serpent. I will remerge again from the sea when *Ragnarök*[41] comes, the final battle between order and chaos. This will happen when all the bonds will break. Like fear and fury, I will contaminate your world with my poison," said *Jörmungandr*.

The voice was high, guttural, and inhuman. In Norse mythology, *Jörmungandr* was a sea serpent, the middle child of the giantess *Angrboða* and *Loki*. According to the Prose Edda, the serpent grew so large that it was able to surround the earth and grasp its tail. When it releases its tail, Ragnarök will begin.

"Apollonius keep calm, I know what to do."

---

[40] *Midgard* is the name for Earth inhabited by and known to humans in early Germanic cosmology, and specifically one of the Nine Worlds in Norse mythology.

[41] *Ragnarök* is a series of events, including a great battle, foretold to lead to the death of several great figures, natural disasters and the submersion of the world in water.

After reassuring him, Valerius Maximus unsheathed the *tintinnabulum*, an amulet used by the Romans to keep away evil spirits. It was a wind chime or assemblage of bells. The strong wind activated it, making the bells ring. The sea monster seemed intimidated by the sound and became even more aggressive in its movements. As a consequence, *Jörmungandr* wriggled dangerously near the ship and its scared crew.

Everything else happened very quickly. The monster's mouth came very close to Valerius Maximus. He crossed his evil eyes. The legionary had never seen anything like that. Nevertheless, he did not hesitate to face the monster, drawing his gladius. Fortunately, that creature could not deliver its deadly attack. A dimensional passage opened up in front of the trireme and some men were sucked into that magical passage. After that, the portal closed suddenly and the *Miðgarðr*'s snake disappeared into the depths of the ocean.

42

The Black Mine: Neither Day nor Night

Gissur was somewhat dazed and confused. He had no idea how he got there into that parallel universe. The Icelandic chieftain was light-years, literally and figuratively, away from his island. After

---

[42] This is a *Smjörhnútur*, a stave used to ensure butter, but it was procured through non-magical means.

looking around, he understood that the Black Mine was not a hospitable place, not the sort of dimension upon which one would expect to find life.

His mind generated question after question, and then he couldn't answer those questions. And what if Thordis did send him there as a form of punishment? Perhaps the Black Mine was something like Purgatory where his soul could be purified from venial sins; as a consequence, he could be also forgiven for all the mistakes he had made in life.

Gissur still couldn't pull all his thoughts back in, but he realized that there wasn't much he could do about the whole bizarre situation. He didn't even like the idea of being considered the chosen one. Malachy mentioned a portal that the *goði* had finally managed to open. What portal did he refer to? And what did Malachy want from him? The elf's response was not long in coming.

"I'll help you regain power in Iceland, but you have to do something for me."

"Alright then, what's the deal?"

"You have to catch a wolf alive," Malachy said, grinning.

"That's all? Then let's do it as soon as possible."

Malachy started laughing. He knew well that Gissur was a superficial man. It would not have been easy to capture that wolf.

"It is not just any wolf, but a huge and ferocious beast. His name is Fenrir."

Gissur shivered as he heard the name. He stood in torment, in an anguish that grew sore upon him. He felt trapped. The clan leader had changed expression, because it was at that moment that he realized the danger. He was certainly aware of the myths of the Norsemen. *Fenrisúlfr* was a monstrous wolf, the son of the demoniac god *Loki* and a giantess, *Angerboda*.

"Don't worry, you won't be alone. Soon the other chosen people will arrive. They will help you in this arduous undertaking."

"I want my men to do it. I fought a thousand

battles with them. I trust them blindly."

"I'm sorry, but your warriors have not been chosen. You'll see, you'll appreciate your fellow ventures."

While the leader of the *Haukdælir* clan was thinking of a possible way out from the difficult situation he had encountered, a magical portal opened up behind him. About twenty soldiers, fully armed, materialized behind him. They were dirty and exhausted. Gissur turned abruptly toward them. Immediately he had the impression that those warriors had fought strenuously against a fearsome adversary. After a while they fell lifeless at the same time one by one. Three of them had survived that slaughter, but they lay on the ground unconscious. Who were those men? Where did they come from? Did they also travelled as Gissur through parallel worlds to reach the Black Mine?

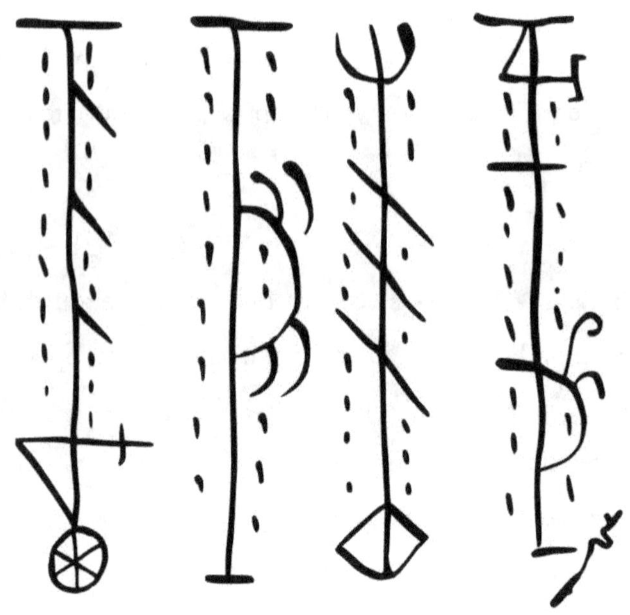

Reykjavík, 4 May 2018 (afternoon)

Let me be clear in my understanding of what was going on in front of me. That encounter was for me like a sort of Copernican revolution in my mind, where all my convictions were surprisingly upset and challenged by new theories. It was like a knowledge surpassing all previous knowledge. Let me be more clear. I do believe in synchronicity. I do think there's something more going on in coincidence, including repeated coincidence, more than meets the eye.

Her name was Gudrun and she was a young girl, incredibly beautiful. My judgement was not purely aesthetic. I very seldom, or perhaps rarely, judge people by what they look like. Therefore, the inner beauty of her soul could not be perceived by superficial and hasty eyes. Then how could I let one unknown girl affect me so much? Perhaps because she was a familiar face.

When I first saw her, she reminded me so much of the same lady that I had met in my dream (or perhaps in the alternate reality?). Yes, they were the same eyes, the same look, the same voice. Indeed, her eyes were magnetic, of a gray-green color; she wore vintage jeans and a sweater that had bizarre and geometric designs; she spoke with a perfect Italian accent. There were too many coincidences for me to call them coincidences.

"Valentino, what's the matter, you look like you've seen a ghost!" Said the mysterious girl.

She looked like she was having fun. Maybe this

was all just a joke my imagination was playing on me.

"How do you know our names?"

"Your aunt Birna is a friend of mine. We worked together in the same department in a clinic for early-detection and enhanced diagnosis of dementias. She phoned me yesterday, telling me that you were interested in the paranormal phenomena that occur in this house. I'm interested too. This seemed like a great opportunity to meet each other. I would also like to check those rumors by personal observation. Furthermore the house belonged to my great-grandfather in the past ..."

"Your great grandfather in the sense that we are all related in Iceland?"

"Very funny! You're good with jokes," replied Gudrun, smiling slightly.

"Where did you learn Italian?" I asked curiously.

"Where do you think I learned it?"

"I don't know, maybe in Bologna?"

"Wrong, I learned it in Naples. My ex-boyfriend lived in an apartment in the historic center. I found myself well in Italy and I will certainly return one day."

So apparently, Gudrun had been living for some time in Naples. This was indeed a surprising proof that could refute my previous convictions about whether I had only imagined, dreamed or met her in an alternate universe. Such an evidence could open a transcendental and philosophical debate of wide proportions. The more I investigated, the more questions kept coming up. I tried to calm down, and I decided not to investigate deeper into the matter, at least not at this point. As the French philosopher and mathematician René Descartes (1596–1650) once said:

I resolved to pretend that all the things that had ever entered my mind were no more true than the illusions of my dreams.

"So what do we do now? Should we go in?" I asked addressing both Marco and Gudrun.

Marco was annoyed by the presence of Gudrun. He didn't expect her to be there waiting for us. I beckoned him to open the garden-gate, and he did. Gudrun followed us, visibly excited. In a few seconds we crossed a weedy garden; then we headed to an old front door. Marco turned the key in the lock and pulled it open. The entrance was barely illuminated by a ray of light coming from a half-open window at the end of a long dark corridor. We were all extremely tense and nervous, but at the same time eager to reveal the secrets behind Solveig's house.

After entering a door at the end of the long dark corridor, we opened a second double-leafed gate. We found ourselves in a large living room, where a piano was covered with a huge green cloth. Finally we opened a third door that led into a kitchen. It was a room furnished with elegant cushioned chairs, sofas, and settees. Then we sat around a table, trying to take stock of the situation.

"Are first impressions always right? My first impression of this place is not good at all. It seems spooky to me," Marco commented.

"I agree with you my friend. I also feel slightly uncomfortable being here," I replied.

"Guys I think it's normal. People said that Iceland's old dwellings all have the same ghostly and oppressive atmosphere that you are feeling now," Gudrun retorted.

I knew what Gudrun was saying was true. Moreover, I heard lots of stories about ghosts and haunted areas from local people. I was disoriented and frightened by how I was feeling. It was also an intriguing situation. Meanwhile, Marco told us about his scary experience that occurred during a vacation weekend.

"A few months ago, my parents and I were traveling to Ischia, a volcanic island in the Gulf of Naples. We stayed at an old house, next to a ruined Roman villa. My room was on the second floor. During the day, after breakfast, I was invited to go to a swimming pool, located not far from the beach and the thermal baths. I wanted to change from my clothes into my swimming suit, so I went to the bathroom to get ready. Without realizing I was also carrying a camera in my pocket. Incidentally, I took some pictures in front of a mirror. After few minutes, my father Paolo asked me to come out quickly because I was taking too long to change clothes. Rushing to be in time, I did not look at these random pictures. Next morning, as soon as I woke up, I was moved to see the images captured the day before. I reached my camera and started to look at them one by one. When I opened one of the pictures, I was shocked. My heart started pounding when my eyes saw a person standing on the glass door as he bowed his head, watching me. He was wearing a white dress and looked very tired and pale. I did not tell anyone, not even my parents. Unfortunately, on my third day there, I was not feeling well. I had fever. Perhaps because I was so scared, and at the same time, I kept what I've seen. Every time I went into the bathroom, I felt like someone was watching me. Despite being a non-religious person, I said the *Our Father* and *Hail Mary Prayer* throughout my stay in the house for my sake. I also did not lock the bathroom door, because it enabled me to get out of there fast."

While he was telling us about this scary experience, a loud noise interrupted his storytelling.

43

7 INTERCONNECTED WORLDS

Reykjavík, 4 May 2018 (evening)

"What happened?"

"Perhaps something has fallen to the floor," said

---

[43] This is a *þjófastafur*, a stave used against thieves.

Gudrun, who seemed calm and detached.

"Well, let's go check," I suggested, trying to sound brave.

I didn't just lie to them, I've been lying to myself too, because I was so scared. My heart restarted beating fast. But this fear was irrational. I took courage and entered the room first. It was big and full of antique furniture, including a series of paintings depicting Icelandic nature. Soon after Marco and Gudrun entered the room. Everything seemed to us to be in perfect order, when suddenly, another noise broke the eerie silence.

"What is going on in this house?"

A painting had fallen off the wall. It appeared heavy, but despite the impact on the parquet, it didn't look damaged. We picked it up and put it on a large oval table. The canvas represented an antique map of Iceland, where sea monsters were the main subjects of it. I thought to myself that the unknown has always been explained through myth and imagination.

The following date and signature were at its bottom:

Hólmavík, 17 July 1268,

Gissur Þorvaldsson

"What a coincidence! You were mentioning Gissur Þorvaldsson before, weren't you?" I asked Marco, surprised.

"Yes, exactly," he confirmed.

I knew there were too many coincidences happening in the same day. It smelled of a set-up. What was Marco trying to tell me earlier? What about the *Gissur's pact*? What if Marco and Gudrun were trying to scare me off? Maybe Gudrun was part of this, maybe not. It was such a strange situation. I decided it was time to confront them.

"I walked right into this," I said, addressing both of them, "stop messing around now, I'm not in the mood for joking. "

"What are you talking about?"

"Stop teasing me! It's enough. You've had your fun. You're just trying to scare me, and I think you did it very well."

"Valentino, I can assure you that I don't know Marco. However, we didn't intend to scare you. I know it sounds strange, but I think Solveig's house is really haunted."

Gudrun had a serious expression on her face that made me feel even more uncomfortable. I felt disoriented and afraid. I was uncomfortable about the fact that I was not so sure now what to believe. Although these were strange and inexplicable coincidences, it was unlikely that Marco and Gudrun were able to perfectly match them. My grandmother Giuseppina often told me that when things go wrong, we must never lose heart, on the contrary we must have faith and not doubt.

"If you want, we can go back to my aunt's house."

"Marco, I do apologize. I am sorry Gudrun. I really can't explain my previous reaction. Maybe I had a panic attack. Please, let's continue our investigation."

"It's okay Valentino. You don't need an excuse. It just happened. Now it's over. Forget about it."

"Sure, let's continue our investigation."

The trust between Marco, Gudrun and me was finally re-established, but the surprises did not end there. Looking again at the painting, I noticed a detail to which I didn't pay attention before. The canvas was signed and dated with the place name "Hólmavík, 17 July 1268" at bottom right. Hólmavík is a village in the western part of Iceland, by Steingrímsfjörður. This town made me think back to the lucid dream I had previously, in which a sect of intellectuals, philosophers and bankers was precisely called the Sorcerers of Hólmavík. It was just another strange coincidence. Gudrun's voice interrupted my thoughts.

"Look, guys. The map now shows sea monsters and other creatures that were not there before."

"It seems that I don't need to believe in the

paranormal to get involved in whatever is happening here…"

We were stunned and bewildered. As I turned to watch carefully these strange figures, my cell phone rang.

"Valentino, welcome back to Iceland. I was waiting for your call yesterday, all right?"

I didn't immediately recognize the person I was talking to. When I was sure it was Jón Magnússon, my doctoral thesis supervisor, I felt soothed, but for a few seconds, I was speechless.

"Hi Jón, sorry if I didn't call you earlier. These were very intense days for me," I replied, justifying myself.

" Don't worry about it. I've been looking forward to seeing you again. I'd like to talk to you about something. Let's meet up. When's good for you? Tomorrow morning?"

"Sure, but I think we should meet later. Maybe at 15:00?"

"Very good, see you then."

The professor greeted me cordially and our investigation resumed.

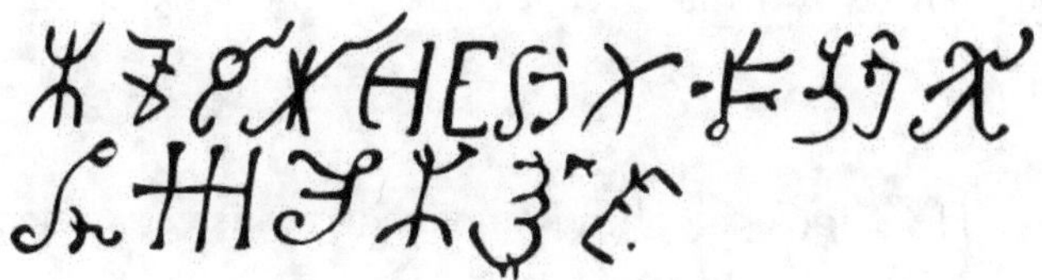

44

Reykjavík, 4 May 2018 (11:00 PM)

By the time I had finished with my phone call, Marco was sitting there watching me with an apprehensive expression on his face. The haunted house was scaring him more than he dared admit to us. He had many questions that he hoped me or Gudrun would be able to answer. How could a painting display what was not there before? Despite his doubts, and despite the anxiety he was feeling in that moment, he forced himself to sit and watch and wait. Then he asked me:

"What do we do now? Should we stay or leave?"

---

[44] This is a *Tóustefna*, a stave used to ward off foxes.

"Marco, we were planning on spending the night out here. If you still agree, I think we should keep that plan."

He shook his head and didn't answer. Then suddenly Gudrun came up with a strange idea.

"Guys, perhaps we should have a séance in this house."

"Are you crazy?" Marco said looking at her disappointed.

A séance is an age-old practice used to make contact with the dead. It has a long history and has occurred in most cultures around the world. Its popularity grew dramatically with the founding of the religion of Spiritualism in the mid-nineteenth century. These kinds of practices would seem to connect mortals with ghosts or other invisible entities.

"What do you think, Valentino?"

"I am not against it. I fear, however, that it may be a dangerous attempt to try communicating with wild spirits. Unless you are an experienced medium, you better not try it."

"I am not an expert, but trust me I know how to do it. I learned from my grandmother and my mother. I was born into a family of psychics. We have all received this gift. We must simply take precautions."

She seemed determined to lead a séance. I had the impression that Gudrun knew how to do it, and so I accepted. In my heart, however, I felt that she was hiding something else.

"If we want to get in touch with a ghost without risks, we need to strengthen our minds and protect ourselves from negative energies. I have some sage incense with me. Its smoke will keep away evil spirits."

"It's disrespectful, the dead should be left in peace!"

"Don't tell me you're afraid, Marco?" Gudrun asked with amusement on her face.

"This isn't about fear, but about respect."

It was not easy to find an agreement between the two. I didn't want to disappoint my friend Marco, but at the same time, I was curious to see "our medium" in action.

"As I told you before, you have to protect yourself psychically, reinforcing minds against negative energies."

"How?"

"First of all, addressing a prayer to the universe, asking it to strengthen our spiritual barriers."

In this regard, I remembered an ancient meditation practice that could be useful to us.

"Some time ago I did an interesting study on shamanism in the Scandinavian countries and I learned a method used by the Druids. This meditative technique consisted of visualizing yourself as a column of white light. Such a display would serve to dissuade certain spirits from performing disruptive actions, or even worse, damage to participants."

"Well, then we can use it as an additional

deterrent to keep unwanted guests away."

Gudrun explained that she would use a divination pendulum and a crystal to ask the spirits some questions.

"This pendulum will help me to tune my life energy with that of the crystal. I will dangle it over the table with slight oscillations once or twice. In this way, if a ghost is available, we will have answers to our questions."

"Gudrun, you're going to need to explain yourself better for us…"

"For example, if we want to ask a ghost about his sex, based on the swing of the pendulum, it will be possible to interpret whether the answer to this question as 'Yes' or a 'No'."

"You're joking, right? Tell me you're not serious."

"Come on Marco, let's at least give it a chance. Will you ever stop being skeptical?"

"I am a rational person, or have you forgotten

that?"

The air was so charged that the tension was palpable. Two friends were fighting (verbally) over rationality and superstition.

"Everyone must agree; otherwise, it could be dangerous," Gudrun admonished.

"Fine. Then let's do it. You know, the story of the pendulum made me laugh. That's all. It reminded me of a not very good magician working on a TV show, during which he was trying to guess, without success, the results of football matches," he said, finally agreeing.

"Perhaps you should apologize to Gudrun."

"There is no need to apologize. Let's begin."

The house was kind of spooky. The atmosphere became eerie.

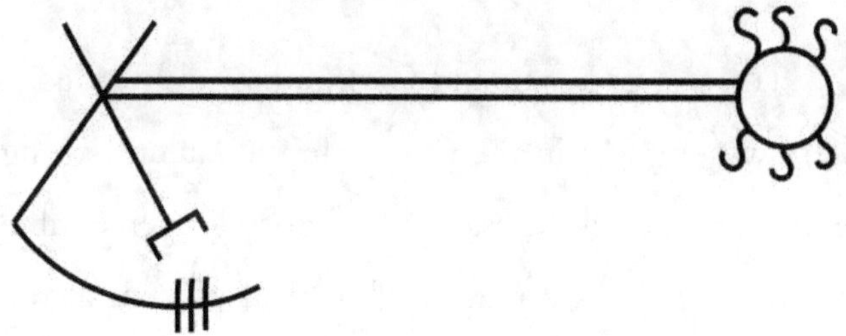

45

8 *SÈANCE*

Reykjavík, 5 May 2018 (midnight)

After the last preparations for the séance, we lit five candles and burned the incense. Finally, we sat around a circular table.

---

[45] This is a *Vatnahlífir,* a stave used for protection against drowning.

We all agreed that to avoid any suggestion, we would have kept our hands together, doing the same with our knees under the table.

The séance began and Gudrun promptly asked if there was a ghost in the room. Her pendulum swung with extreme slowness and almost imperceptible motion. This meant that no ghost was present at the moment.

After a few minutes of fruitless attempts, Gudrun asked again if anyone was listening. Although there were no open windows or drafts in that old salon, inexplicably the flames of the candles began to sway.

Then the candles went out. After turning them back on, Gudrun asked if the spirit could show a stronger sign of his presence. Suddenly the door behind him burst open.

Initially, we had the feeling the door had not been closed properly. Then I got up and closed it again, making sure this time it wouldn't open easily.

Resuming the séance, Gudrun repeated the same request for a more clear sign. The door swung open, but this time the room filled with a strong smell of Sulphur as if that entity wanted to confirm its presence. Marco and I were terrified by the signs shown by the ghost, and we proposed to interrupt the session.

"Now we can't stop," she said in a voice that put a certain fear and began to question the spirit again.

"Who are you? Please answer my question. Who are you?"

But when this same question was repeated several times, in the end, something incredible and at the same time disturbing happened.

All of a sudden, in fact, colored lights materialized in the room and took the form of a beast. It was not clear if it was the head of a wolf or a bear. However, those lights quickly disappeared from the room. Marco and I were astonished.

Despite all these inexplicable events that alarmed us a lot, our medium continued undaunted in her evocative activity. She jumped up from the table and took something from her backpack.

"This is an *Ouija* board, on which all the letters of the alphabet are drawn, the numbers from 0 to 9, a "Yes" and a "No", and other esoteric symbols. It is used for mediumistic communications."

Marco carefully touched his eyelid; his face was a mixture of discomfort and fear, but it was too late to back off. I too let myself be swept away by events.

Resuming again the séance, with the help of the *Ouija* board, the spirit was asked for a further sign. Yet at that moment, which seemed suspended in time, we heard a really loud noise coming from under the table as if someone was knocking against a wall.

Gudrun asked that entity to reveal who he was. By lightly placing the forefinger of her right hand on the indicator, it moved on the *Ouija* board and composed the following sequence of words:

Malachydarkelfsblackmine

"These letters are completely disconnected and meaningless," Marco asserted, looking steadily in my eyes.

"You are wrong. The meaning that can be drawn from these words seems obvious to me. We are dealing with Malachy, a dark elf from a place called the Black Mine," Gudrun said coldly.

Given the successes of our medium in contacting the spirit, both Marco and I were worried about that situation, also because it was getting out of hand. I was also alarmed by the fact that Gudrun was not at all an improvised medium as she had told us at the beginning, but more like an expert clairvoyant. This scared me so much. Generally, when we are faced with inexplicable phenomena we always speak of irrationality. In this case, it was all so real.

"So Malachy, do you have something to tell us?" Gudrun cut him short.

That entity said something that we could not decipher at that juncture. In fact, in the room, a faint voice was heard as if from beyond the grave.

"I don't understand you, can you repeat?"

Gudrun was pressing him as she continued to frantically move the pointer on the *Ouija* board. It was an absurd circumstance. The first voice became stronger. Then the spirit pronounced these cryptic phrases:

Your life is hanging by a thread that can be severed at any moment.

Your soul, on the other hand, is eternal and indestructible.

Which one of you is ready to relive it or to abandon it forever?

I instinctively began to make reflections on life and destiny. My grandmother Giuseppina often said that living is a bit like playing a part without knowing the script. Like entering a house and not knowing what is inside. In that place, you could have nice or unpleasant experiences. Each of us can improvise, however, we are the only ones who in the end decide what to do during these unpredictable events but known by God in advance.

I have often asked myself the question of whether there was a life after death. The soul that is in us where does it go?

For the ancient Egyptians, Greeks, and Romans, the dead continued to live inside the tomb, which for this reason became the final residence of the deceased. For Christians, there would be three options: Hell, Purgatory or Paradise.

Professor Jón Magnússon had a theory about it, according to which we humans are on planet Earth for a variable period following various reincarnations. At the moment of passing away and immediately after death, we would go to the afterlife and from there we would go back to Earth. Those who have reincarnated a few times during this cycle would not long remain in the underworld, while those who have often reincarnated would spend a longer period before returning.

The souls who have not been able to reach the divine light and have not evolved would remain blocked between the afterlife and the Earth. These spirits are those that we mortals call ghosts and that can cause us problems by infesting homes and other places. The souls who have completed the cycle of reincarnations would then pass to a higher level of their existence, a sort of "waiting room", where they would patiently await the other members of their group.

According to Jón, Siddhartha Gautama for example, better known by the name of Buddha, would have been the last of his group and therefore more evolved, as provided of the experiences accumulated during the previous reincarnations by all the other traveling companions. Completed his earthly mission, he would join them in that "waiting room", and then move together to the next unknown level.

From an evolutionary point of view, again according to the theory of the professor, the elves and the hidden creatures would find themselves in an existential level inferior to ours.

Meanwhile, Gudrun continued with her questions, as if she were talking to a real person who lives and breathes:

"What do you intend to tell us? Why did you get in touch with us?"

Those questions were followed by a further enigmatic response from Malachy, whose meaning escaped me. Despite this, his words remained impressed in my memory:

You, Valentino, have been a Hellenist, while Marco was a valiant jarl.

Gudrun, you, however, were always the same.

The elf was taking over our minds and began to give us specific instructions.

You humans can't travel through parallel universes.

I will make your way and you will follow me.

Close your eyes, shake hands and look from the inside on the eyelids.

We were all three absorbed, listening to that persuasive voice. I had a distinct feeling that we could no longer resist him. It was as if everything was moving in slow motion or even as if the clocks had stopped. A sense of anguish invaded my heart and mind. Then something happened of an even more supernatural level, which transcended the limits of imagination.

"Where we are? Guys, I'm afraid."

9 THE OTHER DIMENSION

Black Mine: the Encounter

The chosen people came to the call of Malachy. In reality, they had no chance to decide whether or not to participate in that mission, as they were brutally catapulted into that obscure dimension.

"Dear mortals who have come here. You are brave and intelligent. For this reason, I have chosen you."

The three men were confused, just as Gissur had been a few minutes before. They were Apollonius of Crete, Polybius of Megalopolis and Valerius Maximus Galba. Two Greeks philosophers and one Roman soldier, along with an Icelandic chieftain and a dark elf. Moreover, they came from different spatial and temporal eras.

"I don't understand, we were on board the *Eos*. I remember a monstrous creature that had attacked us. It was hideous and evil. Where are we now? Are we dead?" Polybius wondered disoriented.

"My friend, I am as shocked as you are, nevertheless we remain calm and try to understand more," said Apollonius, showing once again that he was a balanced person, despite being in an unlikely situation.

Valerius Maximus looked into his eyes. His gaze was the same as ever. Proud and intense and. He was a Roman legionary and therefore ready for any eventuality, even the most absurd and unlikely.

"Are we at Thule?"

"This is the Black Mine, the realm of black elves. My name is Malachy and I am the head of the *Døkkálfar*. If you accept to participate, let's say, in a hunt, you will return to your homes safe and sound. I can be generous and I know how to be very bad at the same time. This will depend on how you face the test of courage and devotion I am about to offer you."

The elf explained their mission in detail. Stopping around a fire that burned in the center of a strange flat rock, Apollonius, Polybius and Valerius Maximus listened to him in silence. Probably, they were not aware of what they had got themselves into.

Gissur was watching Apollonius, Polybius and Valerius Maximus, and staying one step ahead of them. He was intrigued by those men who looked so incredibly different from him.

"These are your weapons. Choose the ones you prefer."

"These would be weapons? Do you want us to hunt down your damn wolf with a stone, a mask, a mirror, a chain, and a book?" Valerius Maximus asked irritably.

"You will soon understand why I chose these objects," replied Malachy smiling.

"I am a soldier and I fought numerous battles alongside Lucius Aemilius Paullus Macedonicus. I am a veteran and I generally accept orders only from my general. This time I will have to make an exception to this rule because I have no other choice," stated Valerius Maximus, looking around to let the two Greeks men knowing his point of view. Then turning to Malachy he said:

"I'll bring you that damn wolf. But one thing is clear though: I trust only my *gladius hispaniensis*!"

"My name is Gissur of the Haukdælir clan and lord of the Valley of the hawks. This halberd was given to me by my father. Before him, it had belonged to my grandfather and my great-grandfather. It was passed down from father to son. This is my weapon."

Malachy watched them with an amused and pleased expression. He knew well that with swords and halberds they would never be able to stop Fenrir's fury.

"Agree. Keep your deadly weapons. You will soon realize that they will be of no use. Now go and come back with what will make you free again."

A luminous fissure opened in the rocky wall, revealing the entrance to what must have been an underground tunnel.

"No, wait, explain yourself better," murmured Gissur, who broke off when he noticed a familiar figure behind him.

"Gissur, my lord."

His bodyguard had come to the Black Mine. He probably had no idea how he got there. Perhaps his soul had reincarnated again. Or perhaps at the point of death, he had reached that parallel dimension to satisfy Malachy's request. His suicide was tragic and suspicious as if an evil entity had taken possession of his body, forcing him to carry out that terrible gesture against his will.

"My lord, I thought I had fallen in battle. I don't understand what happened. I don't remember anything."

Gissur cast a defiant look at the elf. He wanted to ask for explanations, but he hesitated. It was Malachy himself who broke the silence.

"I am not involved in his suicide. Many events are unexplainable, but believe me, the death of Magnus had nothing to do with me," said Malachy in a slow, grim tone.

Gissur had a strong suspicion that the black elf was not telling him the truth. However, the Black Mine was not the right place to investigate what were the causes and who were the culprits of that horrible death. Now, they were all victims of something so much bigger than themselves.

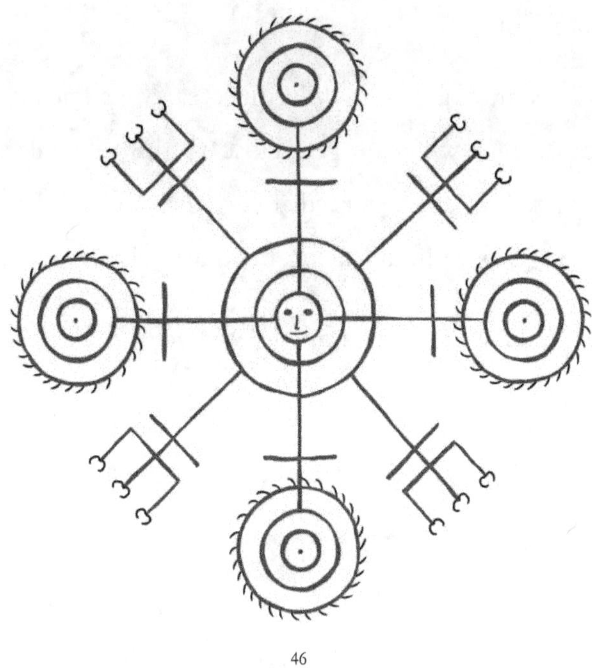

46

Lake Ámsvartnir: The Wolf's Den

The five mortals and Malachy crossed the tunnel
and arrived a few hours later in front of a huge
underground lake, called *Ámsvartnir*. The name
literally meant "pitch black". Its waters were dark but

---

[46] This is a *Veiðistafur*, a stave used for luck in fishing.

transparent, and in some places, they even became very deep.

"Fenrir was last seen in this area. My advice is to capture him when he gets close to drink," Malachy suggested, and immediately disappeared into nothingness without leaving any trace behind.

"Where did that damned dwarf go?"

"Apollonius, I don't like this situation at all. I have to admit that I am afraid," said Polybius.

Magnus was also intimidated and threatened by the decadent atmosphere he was feeling in that timeless dimension. There was a brief debate between the five men on whether it was smart to use the objects provided by Malachy. Apollonius was certain that they were the only effective weapons against Fenrir. Polybius had no opinion about it. Gissur and Valerius Maximus wanted to face Fenrir with sword and halberd. Magnus, despite being a Viking warrior, had sensed that using traditional weapons would only compromise the few "chances" to return safely to their respective historical eras. He also recalled that he had already seen a similar scene in the dream he had before the battle of Örlygsstaðir. Consequently, he feared that without a precise strategy, Gissur and Valerius Maximus could end up like the warriors of his nightmare. Then he analyzed the artefacts and after a few moments of reflection, he spoke to the group.

"You don't know me and I don't know you. We have arrived here for a very short time, but I feel that we must remain united and trust each other. We have a business to accomplish together. We were chosen to capture Fenrir. I believe these five objects could save our lives, so I invite you to listen to me carefully."

According to Magnus, the mask and the stone were meant to scare and distract the beast. The mirror would have served to dazzle his eyes, the chain to immobilize him, and to make his reaction harmless. The book had only one written page. It was a kind of magic formula to be repeated until Fenrir had finally calmed down.

"So is everything clear to you?"

Everyone nodded. Immediately afterward he assigned to each of them the objects. Polybius got the mask; Gissur received the stone; the mirror was for Valerius Maximus, and the chain was for Apollonius. Magnus took the book.

Suddenly Apollonius saw in the distance a monstrous figure proceeding slowly near the lake shore. It was certainly Fenrir. The waters had become murky. Strangely that infernal creature had not noticed their presence, or so it seemed. The beast was now very close. Fenrir first noticed Polybius, who in the meantime had worn the mask. It was a bird mask, used by druids to frighten evil spirits during propitiatory rituals. The wolf seemed terrified and after a while, he started talking to him.

"Thule will be your grave if you continue this journey. You must be careful to investigate whatever is hidden in the darkness. The Romans are demons, and they will be defeated one day."

Polybius was not surprised by those words of warning, but he was certainly alarmed. Indeed he remembered perfectly that in his nightmare Fenrir had told him the same things.

"What if everything is predetermined? If so, where is our "free will"? " He thought to himself.

At that precise moment Gissur, leaning with a knee on a rock, threw the stone. The wolf, struck in the head, turned and began to run rather angry towards the opposite side of the shore. From his position, Valerius Maximus whistled long and sharply, catching the devilish gaze of Fenrir. The wolf god was now close to the Roman legionary. When he saw his image reflected in the mirror, he stood for a moment with his eyes wide open. The moment was propitious and Magnus recited the following magic formula three times:

Vivid dreams will eventually open gates.

Vivid dreams will eventually open gates.

Vivid dreams will eventually open gates.

Fenrir then became calm and meek. Apollonius hastened to chain him, while he was still in a state of semi-unconsciousness.

The legs were quickly immobilized by the group of heroes who came to the aid of the Cretan. Once chained, the beast recovered control of its body and tried several times to bite the humans. A few feet from the jaws of the wolf god, only a few feet from the shore, a tiny golden object began to vibrate and frantically zigzag in the heavy air of the lake *Amsvartnir*, like a shining mad insect. Its movement described gaps in space. With each new movement, the tears were joining together, to create a void that moment by moment expanded magically, eventually creating a dazzling rectangle. It was the portal. The monster's fangs were a short distance away and the five chosen feared that the much-needed salvation was not so easy to achieve. Even if the monster could not move its colossal legs, it was still free to tear them to pieces. If only they had come close enough to that escape route. Suddenly the other four objects received by Malachy joined together and shaped something extraordinary that definitively immobilized Fenrir's jaws. He made in vain the most violent efforts to break loose.

Thus, Apollonius, Polybius, Valerius Maximus, Gissur and Magnus immediately disappeared, sucked into the portal. Their mission had been accomplished.

10 EVERY PHANTOM, A DESTINY

Rome, the General's *domus*

The triumph was the highest reward for a Roman general. Finally, the old leader could receive honors for his amazing military exploits. This was the peak of his career. But not everyone agreed with that consecration. Many of his veterans were dissatisfied because they had received only a meagre reward in exchange for their loyalty and self-sacrifice during the campaign against King Perseus. In the end, despite some heated protests in the Senate, the elders voted in favor of the triumphal march. The festivities lasted for three whole days.

Before and after the celebration, Paullus's soul was disturbed by tragic events: two of his four sons died in mysterious circumstances. Both were found with a dagger stuck in their chest. Word had spread that the general was the victim of a curse whereby his family members had to die a violent death. But there was something else that tormented him more and more. He wanted to reveal the secrets of Thule, the legendary island, mentioned in the travel journals of the Greek explorer Pytheas.

The same evening, after the public funeral of his sons, celebrated with great pomp in the forum, Paullus had two Greeks summoned, who had become prisoners following the victorious battle of Pydna.

"I have an assignment for you. If you accept my proposal, you will be free to return to your own homes. But if you do not accept it, I guarantee that the rest of your life will be hard. Very hard."

"My lord, we are very grateful and honored for the opportunity. What is it about?"

"Greeks are extraordinary sailors and your colonies were founded everywhere. I need you for an important mission on behalf of the people and the Senate of Rome. You will set sail from Massalia aboard a trireme."

"But we are not sailors my lord. Apollonius is a philosopher and I a historian. We know nothing about navigation or how to establish a colony."

"Your past experiences and your intellectual capacities make both of you the right choice for this mission. Apollonius, I'd like to nominate you as the ambassador of the Roman Republic to Thule. Polybius, you will be responsible for writing a journal of the voyage. You will have to reach the island of Thule, like the Greek navigator Pytheas did before."

Polybius was shocked to hear what Paullus said. He had the strange sensation of having already experienced that scene. And besides, he knew inexplicably that this journey would be disastrous. He had clear memories of his previous expedition in search of Thule. And he could not understand why he vividly remembered having even found himself catapulted into another dimension in the presence of an elf named Malachy and a demigod wolf named Fenrir.

How could he explain to Paullus something that not even he fully understood?

"We are delighted by your proposal, my lord, but I don't think it would be a good idea," replied Apollonius.

Polybius looked at him surprised, then realized that also his fried had experienced the same incredible journey.

"How dare you contradict me! I advise you not to take advantage of my benevolence."

"General, the Greek slave is right," intervened Valerius Maximus, "this journey would only cause misfortune and disaster."

Paullus was astonished. He could not bear to be contradicted. However, he was also superstitious and for this, he was struck by the words of his bodyguard.

" Why are you saying that?"

The Greeks men and the Roman soldier looked into each other's eyes. After a moment's hesitation, Polybius stepped forward.

"My lord, the truth is that Thule's discovery, namely the island described in Pythea's diary, never actually occurred. It was an imaginary journey. "

"Yes, but how do you know?"

"My father was the commander in chief of the Achaean League, as well as the most eminent man of Megalopolis. One day he commissioned me to discover the authenticity of Pythea's writings."

"What did you find out? Why do you think they are fake?"

"They are not fake. On the contrary, these are extraordinary documents."

"You are making a fool of me? If they are not false, why did you say before that Pythea had imagined everything?"

Paullus was getting nervous with Polybius and thought he was a cheeky liar. But there was something strange, he could not understand. Even Valerius Maximus, his most trusted man, was supporting the Greek slaves. He was convinced that it might be worth listening to that story to the end.

"There are dimensions parallel to ours, where time and space merge, becoming detached from each other. Thule is one of these places my lord. Places inhabited by the 'hidden people', creatures that can be dangerous for us mortals."

"General, I understand how surreal this thing is. Believe me, it would be better to give up such a feat," admonished Valerius Maximus.

The elderly leader was perplexed and lost in the face of such impudence. Then he remembered the vision he had during a propitiatory rite when he was part of the College of the Augurs.

In that vision, he was on an unknown island in the company of two castaways. One of them spoke to him of the "hidden people". The other castaway told him instead that the power of the wolf-god could guarantee the Romans an incredible power. He linked the two stories and only then realized that the premonition he had previously had another meaning.

"Paullus, you must be careful to investigate whatever is hidden in the darkness," said a persuasive and hypnotic voice.

He understood at that moment that Thule was nothing more than a place to avoid, for his own sake, and for Rome's sake. However, it was too late. The successes of his political and military career were thus not accompanied by a happy family life.

Örlygsstaðir, 22 August 1238

"Dear Gissur, I wonder if you know where you're going?"

The leader of the *Haukdælir* clan remembered very well what would have happened to his best warrior straight after. Suffering from anxiety he had never felt before, Gissur ran to him, who was ready to extract his dagger to commit suicide. With a great blow on his head, he disarmed Magnus. The warrior woke instantly from the trance state and asked his boss the reasons for that hostile gesture.

"Why did you slap me?"

"My friend, I only saved your life."

"I feel like I've woken up from a mead hangover."

He needed a few moments to bring back the memory of the Black Mine, Malachy, Fenrir and the other men from the past. Then he remained silent, trying to figure out if there was a logical connection between the battle of Örlygsstaðir and the trip to the Black Mine. Gissur interrupted that silence.

"In the other dimension, someone told me that we travelled through universes parallel to ours. It is a dimension that is not perceptible to our senses but it exists."

"So it was not a dream, but my lord a prodigy?"

"There are human beings, like you and I

apparently, capable of perceiving and interacting with these parallel worlds."

Suddenly a figure appeared from nowhere. She was a woman with long white hair she held in braids, wrapped around her head like a crown. His skin was pale.

A sense of terror pervaded Gissur. He had recognized her despite the confusion generated by the succession of events. A disturbing smile appeared on Thordis's face.

"When one is convinced that destiny does not exist, one is led to believe that it is possible to change it. But fate from a favorable standpoint, it can always become adverse."

The witch closed her eyes and began to recite the same rhyme:

Now let's see if you understand this.

Why the sun and the moon live in the sky?

The foolish men are always anxious for justice.

A monstrous wolf will rise against you.

Traitor, exterminator.

Who will save you now?

No one is coming to save you.

Gissur and Magnus were paralyzed and eventually lost consciousness. Meanwhile, a strange creature materialized on the scene, grabbed Gissur's arm and released him from the spell.

"Although I cannot save both, the pacts must always be respected."

Malachy did not forget the agreement he had made with Gissur. Magnus' fate was different instead. He fell into a deep sleep, and he would never wake up again.

Reykjavík, 6 May 2018

"Everything is dark here."

That place was surrounded by the thickest and darkest night. Gradually I was enveloped by a dazzling white light that soon brought everything back to normal. It was as if I had just seen a movie with a pair of 3D glasses. More precisely, it was like a reality show I watched as a spectator. Then a hand touched my shoulder.

"Valentino, are you okay?" I realized that Marco was sitting next to me.

He was visibly shaken, even though he had first become acquainted. We immediately realized that Gudrun was gone.

"Do you want to see that I imagined it again?"

"Not at all. I was also in that dimension together with you," Marco confirmed, "and I remember that Gudrun performed a séance as a medium."

Yeah, but where had Gudrun gone? We looked everywhere, but Gudrun was nowhere to be found. We started to get worried.

"She is probably gone."

"What a strange night. Yet it all seemed so real."

"I told you, Valentino, I was with you and I remember everything: the meeting with Gudrun, the séance, the elf called Malachy, our trance and the enterprise of the five chosen."

That morning the surprises were not over. We noticed that the sea monsters, the signature "Hólmavík, 17 July 1268", and the dedication to Gissur Þorvaldsson had disappeared from the painting. A phone call, this time on Marco's cell phone, interrupted our conversation.

"How was the night in the haunted house?" Birna asked.

"Aunt Birna, I will tell you, but, first of all, could you tell me where Gudrun lives?"

"Who?"

"The girl you sent to us and who worked with you last summer at the hospital."

"What are you talking about? I don't think I know her," she replied, amused," by chance have you already started to kill hearts?"

Marco answered with a sentence of circumstance and greeted his aunt.

"See you later Birna!"

"*Ciao bello*, see you!"

This worried me a lot, as it confirmed what I had feared from the beginning. Gudrun existed not only in my imaginative mind but also as an incorporeal presence. All happenings should be taken in one's stride, in an unmitigated and unruffled, calm manner. However, it was very difficult to fully understand, but she was a ghost that haunted me, perhaps because of my interest in the occult. Well, I don't want to sound negative, but I am sure of one thing, this entity will continue to show up in the future.

47

Reykjavík, the Day of "Right Choices"

After a year spent in Iceland, Cristian had found
the job he wanted at an Icelandic bioengineering

---

[47] The Christogram IHS is a monogram symbolizing Jesus
Christ. From Greek it is an abbreviation of the name ΙΗΣΟΥΣ
(Jesus).

company. He even met a good Polish girl named Lena, with whom he began a romantic love story. As far as I am concerned, I accepted the offer made by Jón as his assistant. That umpteenth experience with the paranormal in *Suðurgata*'s villa had changed my approach to the subject. I decided that it was better to leave the investigation of Icelandic elves and ghosts for a while. I then began interesting research on Scandinavian Catholics. Thanks to these new studies, I remembered the words of Father Santoro, on which I reflected for a long time.

"You must be careful to investigate whatever is hidden in the darkness."

Father Santoro was right about the meaning of life: its meaning is the journey itself, a unique experience that should not be wasted searching for answers from the occult.

When he passed away, I realize how important he was to me. I missed especially our long chats and his wise reflections. He was a member of the Society of Jesus, a religious order of the Catholic Church founded by Ignatius of Loyola. I would like to share with you his last words about the "right choices" in life, written on a memorial card a few months before his death.

I am convinced that I hit the right target, I didn't miss the shot: I chose well, I chose Jesus.

Or rather Jesus chose me, I didn't ignore his call, I answered it: I want to imitate you, I want to be like you, I want to do what you did. More than sixty years after that call, I am more than satisfied, convinced that I have found the hidden treasure, the precious pearl.

But Jesus is the universal man, he belongs to everyone, even to you; entrusts to all a mission, a service to be disengaged in life.

The discontent of many people is due to the lack of conscious choices, motivated by reasons of faith, which constitute an ideal.

The diploma, the degree, the best job position cannot be enough, they do not fully satisfy.

Many people at the age of decisions did not ask themselves what the Lord wanted from them, they did not ask him. I asked myself and I feel a great privilege; I am enthusiastic about my vocation; I do not finish thanking the Lord, asking myself: why this fate has touched me. If I had to start over I would do the same choice with my eyes closed.

I wish relatives and friends to know what I feel at the end of a long life consecrated to the exclusive service of God.

Father Gioacchino Santoro (1911-2007)

ABOUT THE AUTHOR

Valerio Gargiulo is an Italian writer of supernatural fiction and fantasy. Gargiulo was born September 26, 1979, in Naples, Italy. He has been active both in the field of legal advice and research. He studied at Reykjavik University and finished his Master of Laws in 2015. Previously, after completing a Bachelor of Laws at University of Naples Federico II, he has been freelancing, drafting reports and legal agreements. He also worked as a preschool teacher and EEG technologist. He self-published his first novel "The Incredible Journey of a Neapolitan Puffin" in 2018.